INSIDE...THE MIND OF A MAN!

INSIDE...THE MIND OF A MAN!

Stacey Green

iUniverse, Inc.
New York Lincoln Shanghai

INSIDE...the mind of a man!

Copyright © 2006 by Stacey Green

All rights reserved. No part of this book may be used or reproduced by any means, graphic, electronic, or mechanical, including photocopying, recording, taping or by any information storage retrieval system without the written permission of the publisher except in the case of brief quotations embodied in critical articles and reviews.

iUniverse books may be ordered through booksellers or by contacting:

iUniverse
2021 Pine Lake Road, Suite 100
Lincoln, NE 68512
www.iuniverse.com
1-800-Authors (1-800-288-4677)

ISBN-13: 978-0-595-39421-0 (pbk)
ISBN-13: 978-0-595-83817-2 (ebk)
ISBN-10: 0-595-39421-3 (pbk)
ISBN-10: 0-595-83817-0 (ebk)

Printed in the United States of America

DEDICATIONS

First and foremost I'd like to thank God for blessing me with the talent to express myself thru my writing ability.

I also want to thank my mom who has prayed for me for many, many years and who encouraged me to write after seeing a few of my early poems.

I want to thank my family, my sister Janet and my brothers Jonathan Jr. and William and last but not least my children, I love you very, very much!

Last but definitely not least I would like to thank my Pastor Jesse Curney III. You've helped me in ways you didn't even know.

Joy L Collins
(678) 428-6442
(770) 892-3909

999.

1994

nch,
chtree

1992

t Corp.

2 in. +

DULT

/5?searchdata1=electronic+basic&srchf... 11/1/2006

1Co 13:11 When I was a child, I spoke like a child, thought like a child, and reasoned like a child. When I became an adult, I no longer used childish ways

Chapter 1

▼

"Go Jay, it's ya birthday!"

By the time I reached 30 my life was just beginning…having spent the past 13 years dropping out of high school, having children, working one factory job after another, womanizing, selling drugs, womanizing, using drugs, robbin' cheatin' and stealin'…to letting go and letting God, getting clean and sober and turning my life over to God…finally for the first time in my life—my life as an adult…. I was opening my eyes to the world.

*With a future unseen, and thoughts of the past
Now with a clear mind things move so fast
So many years of disgust
So much hurt, so much pain
Not just inflicted on myself, but also on others, for no gain.

My selfish ways did not faze me
Not even a thought did occur
13 years would move so fast, it just happened
Like a blur

What can I do to make this right?
It's my 30th birthday, the party's tonight
I give thanks to you my Jesus for showing me wrong from right
And for blessing me the 10,950 days of my life*

(phone rings) Hello—"What's up Jay, tonight's the night baby boy! Figured out where we're going yet?" "Maybe we can catch a Bingo game or something! Isn't that what old people do?" Darryl was a joker—class clown, always was, always will be. I've known him since the 9th grade. That's when we first began getting in trouble. Cutting class, hanging out, we've been thru the jungle together, and thank the Lord, we both made it out alive with no prison record, no bullet holes, and no knife wounds. OK, so maybe a knife wound here or there! I was once cut with a butterknife by one crazy chick, but that's another book. Basically, we grew up.

"Man, I really need to be going to church to thank God for keeping me for 30 years, but I don't think he is going to be angry if I go in search of my future wife tonight."

You must understand, I knew nothing about commitment. Hell, I don't even know that I know now, but I know what I want. I'm learning what God has intended for me. I just gotta make it happen. Already with two children and no stable home life, major changes needed to be made. I was never the type to be faithful to anything other than what I wanted, what I needed, what made ME feel good. Unable to face life on its own terms, I chose to hide behind people, places, and things.

"There's a hot new Jazz joint on the West End I've heard about, let's go check that out" I said to Darryl. "Man you're my boy not my boo!" We're going to a REAL club." "Let's go to the city," he said "Cool!" "Meet me at my house around eleven."

"Yo man, what's taking you so long?" I asked. "It's 11:30! You told me to be here at 11:00!" If it was one thing I couldn't stand about my boy D was that he was ALWAYS late. *"Yo, I'm about to go without you! Meet me there,"* I yelled to him from his living room. *"Man hold one second, I ran out of toilet paper and had to cut up an old shirt! Now the toilet is overflowing!"* That was Darryl for you. About an hour later, homeboy came out decked out in a suit, tie, hat...the whole nine, smelling like he jumped into a tub of cool water cologne right before he walked out the bathroom. You couldn't tell him HE wasn't the man. Me on the other hand, I was more casual...slacks, fitted silk pull over shirt with a rounded collar and a blazer with some ole skool Stacy Adams on, smelling much more intriguing than nauseating.

I would say I am a rather good looking brother. 6'2", medium built, light-skinned, straight short hair with long eyelashes...a pretty boy some would call me. I never had a problem attracting a woman. That is what partly would keep me in so much trouble in my younger years.

Darryl was a nice looking guy as well, even though us brothers aren't really allowed to say such things, so you didn't hear that from me! No down-low brother here! He's about 6'2 medium built, a little darker than me and has a bald head, but he was flashy with his. It usually worked well when we were together because usually a woman would want one or the other...cute & flashy or sexy & reserved. I guess you could say together we were like Burger King...have it your way! But tonight it was different. It was my 30th birthday and I didn't want a casual fling...I wanted LOVE! This is about beginning a new chapter in my life.

I believe life has (4) chapters-(4) quarters for you sports buffs:
1st chapter—
Adolescence, you learn-grow-make mistakes, realize your mistakes, and hopefully learn from your mistakes. Here you still have time to right the wrongs, to begin your plan, then onto chapter 2.

2nd chapter—
(if you're lucky enough to survive chapter 1)...chapter 2 is about getting serious-taking off the masks and revealing who you really are. Going AFTER life instead of waiting for life to find you.
3rd chapter—
By now you should be happily married, financially stable, goals have been met and now you are reaping the rewards! Enjoying the fruits of your labor and preparing for the 4th and final chapter.
4th chapter—
CHILLIN'—you and your spouse are growing old together...grandchildren coming around, traveling, seeing the world, no more work-stress or anything major to do. Going to Bingo! Basically riding off into the sunset!

Tonight began Chapter 2!

"Yo man, I didn't want to tell you this until we got here, but this chick I work with that I've been dying to get at is coming here tonight and she has a girlfriend!"
"I understand it's your birthday and all, and I want you to be happy! Believe me, I saw the pictures of her and she is bad! Trust me!" When Darryl flashes that "trust me" smile, generally it would mean "aw man, I really didn't know," but tonight he was right on point!

I saw the look on his face as they came thru the door. We were standing at the bar, about to order a coke and I saw his face when these two women walked up to us. I would have chosen either one, but the shorter of the two kept my attention. "Jay, this is my co-worker Karen, my boo! (blowing kisses), and ladies this is my boy Jay, its Jay's birthday today!" "Well, happy birthday Jay" said Karen. "Darryl said you were nice looking (oops, I forgot he told me not to tell you that!). This is my girlfriend Brianna. We've known each other since grade school." Brianna was the shorter of the two and the one my eyes were glued to from the very beginning. "Well, happy birthday Jay." "Thank you beautiful!" "Thank you for coming to celebrate it with me! I didn't ask for a present, but OK!"

Brianna was gorgeous! She was about 5'4", slim up top with lovely hips and beautiful bow legs. She had on this short little skirt with a slight split up the right side of her right thigh. She was a little lighter than I and her hair was cut in this cute short funky hairstyle. Nails were primed and polished, toes done with a little toe ring on her left 2nd toe, and had a smile that would make the sun jealous! "It's a real pleasure to meet both of you." I took Brianna by the hand, "let's find a table." Truth be told, I would have stood in the middle of the floor butt naked in a room full of midgets as long as she was there with me!"

As I lead her to find a table, out of the corner of my eye I could see Darryl with this great big grin on his face. He knew my taste, he knew my style of woman. Often he would envy me with my choices, and as it seemed "luck" of the women I had in my life, but I would always manage to blow it. In my eyes, no woman was ever good enough for my heart. There was Theresa, Lynn, Lisa, and Tracey. All beautiful women inside and out, but with each one I could give you a reason, an excuse, why it didn't work. "Man I would pay to have just ONE of your ex's!" Darryl would tell me often. His luck with women was not too good. He would meet women that were real 'drama queens' or either had much 'baby daddy drama' going on. Too much for me!

He wanted to love and could not meet a decent woman. Me-I had the beautiful, successful, single, no children women but either I didn't want to or I didn't know how to love, but that was then. Little did I know it would be that night, on my 30th birthday, my life-my views on love and marriage, my feelings on monogamy and being faithful in a relationship all would change because of this one woman.

"This is a really nice place, do you come here often?" Brianna asked. "Actually, we haven't been here in a minute" I said. "Yeah, the last time we were

here you left me when that chick...what's her name?...." *Darryl could sense by the look I gave him that then was not the time for that story.* "Have either of YOU ever been here?" *I asked Brianna and Karen.* "No, but someone in my business circle told me it was a hot spot," *Brianna said.* "Oh really, what line of work are you in?" "I'm in the entertainment industry!" "Really?" *I asked,* "in what way?" "Let's just say I help people reach their dreams!" *All the while I was thinking, 'man, I would love for you to help me reach mine!'* "Ok.... OK *(nodding my head in approval)* "Do you work for yourself or for a company?" "I'm freelance" "So you're like a manager of sorts?" "Yes, I guess you can say that" "Do you deal with anyone famous?" *Darryl chipped in* "maybe you can introduce me to Martin Lawrence or Chris Tucker. Hell anyone for that matter! I'm the next great up and coming stand up comedian," *he said as he cracked a silly smile.* "I really only deal with musical talent" *Brianna responded.* "You just don't wanna hook a brother up, but that's cool Bri!" *We all started laughing.* "So, what line of business are you in Mr. Jay?" *she asked.* "I'm Vice President of Operations for an internet security firm here in Manhattan by day and I freelance as a ghost writer in my spare time." "Wow! I'm impressed" "Yeah, me too!" *Darryl chipped in.* "You are so silly!" *Karen said to Darryl.* "He is like this all day at work. That's why I can't take him seriously!" "Can't take me seriously?" "OK Karen, you want serious?
I seriously want to suck on your cheek!" *Everyone busts out laughing.* "What's so funny? I told you I was serious!" "Ya boy got issues!" *Karen said.* "Oh he's fine now, You should have seen him when we were younger!" *I said.*

I took Brianna by the hand *"come on, let's dance."* Very willingly she took my hand and allowed me to lead. Just as we reached the dance floor, the music changed from hip-hop to Luther Vandross. She looked embarrassed as I took her arms and placed them on my shoulders. Gently I wrapped my arms around her waist. I tried to be a gentleman about it, but I wanted her as close to me as possible! I pulled her into me and buried my nose in the top of her hair. Even her hair smelled good! Freshly washed with Strawberries and cream shampoo. "Ummm, you smell so good" she said." "What are you wearing?" "You, right now!" She looked at me and smiled. "Oh my goodness!" My heart melted right underneath my shirt, down my leg and onto the dance floor! She had the prettiest eyes you could ever imagine! I lost all train of thought as I drifted into her eyes…

*Ever since I was young, I've had a romantic dream. I'd have some incredible woman who'd knock me off my feet, and we'd live happily ever after. We'd settle down somewhere quiet, a place that we could call home. We'd have kids, a dog, and a big backyard…a home filled with love and laughter. For a long time, I thought this dream would never come true. The real world often falls short of our fantasies, but when I met you, I had no idea that I had found what I've been praying for. When I think about looking into your eyes, you would drift out of my dreams and into my reality. Now I feel that my life is nearly complete. There's only one thing missing…. I need to know if you feel this way too. Are you willing to make this dream come true? I can honestly tell you that I want nothing more than to spend the rest of my life with you.

When you love someone, you'll do anything, even things you can never imagine doing. You'll fly to the sky and steal a star…you'll keep loving them despite your many scars. You'll believe a lie and swear it's the truth…you'll stay faithful through the lonely nights, despite the maddening loneliness. You'll cherish the pain in your heart and soul, and nothing will change your mind. You'll sacrifice your mind, body, and soul…your whole life; you'll do it and you won't think twice. You'll simply bandage your wounds and fly to the moon when the one you love is in sight.

Even though we both may be mindful of the past…past hurts, past loves…. I feel we could make a new start. Together. Every night now when I close my eyes and dream about you, imagining how great it would be if we were together. Imagining what could be. I know we can make it together. I have faith in you and our love for each other.

I know I'm not perfect, but I care so much for you and I think it's time that I confessed all.
I want to lie…lie in bed with you and hold you close to me.
I want to cheat…cheat on our budget and my diet in order to have an exciting fun-filled weekend with you, just you and me and a lot of you know what!
I want to steal…steal time away from our busy day, work and any other of my responsibilities so that I can spend quality time with you.
I want a divorce…to divorce myself from all of my worries and fears, and focus entirely on you and our future together.
Yes, I confess. I love you and all I want is to be with you.

Don't be afraid to bare your soul and tell me what you think about our chances together. Whatever you decide, I swear that I'll always love you and will always be committed to you and our time together whether past, present or future. I've been in love before, but never the way I plan on loving you. My heart is true, and now I'm just waiting to begin my life with you*.

"Jay…Jay! Uh…the music is fast again!" I snapped back into reality. "We've been dancing for three slow songs and one fast one already. I didn't want to disturb your flow so I figured I'd let you go on but I'm getting tired sweetie!" "I'm sorry, I just had this wonderful fantasy!" "If it didn't include me, I am going to be really upset," she said. "Sorry, I can't tell you that yet, but just know that it definitely wasn't about anyone else." We enjoyed the rest of the evening…together! We really appeared to be a couple that had been together for years. It was a wonderful night!

Chapter 2

The fellas

"Yo, what happened to YOU last night?" Darryl asked. "After you and Brianna came back from the dance floor, both of you were like—gone!" "What do you mean gone?" I asked. "I tried to talk to you all night playa!" "Every time I said something to you, you were looking at her with that look of lust in your eyes! Her too for that matter!" "You finally came through for a brother! It's about time!" I said. Usually, it would be one of my girlfriends that would hook HIM up. I was always putting him down on one of my girlfriends—girlfriend. "Yeah man, Bri is a STAR!" I said emphatically. "I can't even tell you what we talked about all night at the club! I'm STILL drunk! It's like I have a hangover when there was no alcohol even close to us! She wants to hook up later on this evening." "I thought we were going to meet Curtis and T-Mac?" Darryl asked "You know we have a meeting tonight." I know what you're thinking...what can a group of grown behind men have regular meetings about? The same thing grown behind women have meetings about, the opposite sex! We would always keep each other informed of where we were in our relationship life, and since two of us were committed, we knew where they were, but where was it going!? It was our way of keeping sane and not allowing the stress of a relationship wear us down. If one of us started 'catching feelings' for a woman and tried to keep it a secret, he would get called out to find out why. He had some splainin' to do (as Ricky Ricardo would tell Lucy). Believe it or not, it was typically constructive advice. Yeah, we would get silly sometimes and lie about seeing one of the others' girl coming out of the strip club with a gym bag or something like that, but mostly we would just 'kick-it'. "I can't tonight man, I'm just gonna have to call them." "and tell them what?" Darryl asked. "That you're going out with a woman you just met and you can't make the meeting?" "You KNOW you are gonna catch heat behind this don't you?" he asked. "I'm telling you now, keep me out of it! Don't even mention my name!"

"Whatever"…that's not where my thoughts were, they were on Brianna. You can best believe I was hoping hers was on me as well. "I'm about to go home man, Bri is coming by around seven and I need to straighten up." "I thought you said you were going out?" Darryl asked. "Are you working for somebody? I replied." "Did someone hire you to get them information on me?" That's what we would say to each other when too many questions were asked. "Let me do me and I will get with you later on." "Cool."

It was a beautiful Saturday afternoon and I had a really good feeling about the day. As a matter of fact, I had a GREAT feeling about the day! I arrived at my house and opened the door. There was note on my floor. How did this get here? All it says is 'check your answering machine.' It smelled like Brianna, but how did she know where I live. Oh yeah, I told her last night. Forgot!
I hit the 'speaker' button on the phone…
(you have 2 new messages) the recording says. (message 1 sent at 12:58pm) "Jay, I thought you were calling me back? You know I need you to come over here and…." "My mom"…(message saved)…(message 2 sent at 1:34pm) "Hey Jay it's Brianna. I just want to tell you that I had a wonderful time last night! I really wish you could refresh my memory about some of the things we talked about. For some reason, I feel like I have a hangover. All I know is that when I woke up, there you were—I saw you, I

smelled you. It scared me because obviously you have been here since I left you last night! I can't wait to see you later on. I should be there around 7…(bye for now)" I MUST BE DREAMING!!! (phone rings)

"Hello" "Jay what's up man, it's me Curtis." "Oh, what's up Curt?" "Darryl called me and said that you couldn't make the meeting tonight! He said you were going out with this female you just met last night!?" "Oh, but he said he didn't want to get involved huh?" "What?" "Never mind man." "Listen, I'll get up with you tomorrow. After church we could hook up, but not tonight." "It's gonna cost you man, you do know that?" "Cool, I got you!" "So who is she?" "Her name is Brianna"—"Yeah, I know that already" "Let me guess…Darryl?" "do you really need to ask?" Curt said. "Look man, I said I don't have time right now. I told you I got you. Let me get back to you OK? Tomorrow, after church."

Curt, T-Mac and I were friends longer than Darryl and I. The three of us grew up together downtown Elizabeth. Our moms would baby-sit each of us, so we had history. They were like brothers to me. Curt has been with his girl for over fifteen years but they were not married. I guess they'd been together so long that it was not even worth the trip down the isle. At least that's how HE felt! They have two children together. Every now and then he would test the waters, but he wasn't going anywhere. I wouldn't say he was happy…he was comfortable!

T-mac went to Purdue University on a football scholarship after high school, but he blew out his knee in his sophomore season. He was a big guy—played defensive tackle so you KNOW he had to be big! He had not long ago hooked up with a young lady himself that he had known for a while. Neither one of them had any children. T-mac was a Q so he would hang out with his frat brothers a lot doing a lot of partying and such, but this new lady of his was quickly changing that. They were even talking about marriage! That was supposed to be one of the topics of the meeting tonight.

What should I do with Brianna tonight? We could go out and get something to eat! Naw, then I wouldn't be able to talk to her too much. Plus, I'm not ready for her to see me grub yet! A movie? Heck no—you don't wanna put someone that beautiful in the dark for 2 ½ hours! That's a crime! Maybe we can go to Atlantic City, walk and hold hands on the boardwalk, then catch a show. That's going to require an overnight stay and we're not at that point yet.
"Got it!" *I'll take her to the NY pier and maybe we could cruise the Hudson. Yeah! Soft music playing, standing on the deck holding her from behind as we circle the Hudson. Water glistening with the back drop of the New York City skyline! Yeah!*

Maybe I should focus on getting this house together. Typically, I'm a very together brother when it comes to my house. Nothing in my house is out of order. To me, a mess means confusion and I don't subscribe to that magazine. I must really like this girl to be blowing off a meeting!
(phone rings) "Hello".... "Brianna, who is Brianna?" "Oh, what's up T-Mac" "skip all that lil' homey, I hear you got a new girl…waaaazzzuuuppp!?"
"I'll put you down tomorrow T at the meeting. I gotta go clean up man." "Ok, Ok, hold on playa. I really called to see where you and she were going tonight?" "Me and Blink might wanna roll." *Blink was his girl. Don't ask why the name Blink. I believe it's because she batted her eyes like 1000 times a minute or something like that, but she was cool.*

She understood 'the fellas' and would never do anything to come between us. "Not tonight T. I just met her last night. Give me SOME time with her alone!" "We all can hang out NEXT weekend," *I tried to explain.* "Oh, you plan on keeping her around for a while huh?" 'Ouch' "Whatever man, I'll get with you later. Peace."

(doorbell rings) *Man, it's 7 already? Luckily I had time to cut my hair, shower and throw on the Dolce & Gabana…REALLY!*

When I opened the door, she was standing there looking like a Ruth Christ Steak…succulent, moist, and ready to eat! Man, did she look casually amazing!
"What's the picnic basket for," I asked. "I figured we'd go to the park. I have a blanket, a few throw pillows, some wine, a little cheese & crackers, a board game (Motown monopoly) and me!" "Cool" I didn't even tell her about MY plans for the evening. Just to see a woman taking charge and planning a romantic day FOR us was impressive! "Come on, we can take my car," she said. In front of my house was a convertible Acura TL and yes, she had the top down. It was late in the evening, but the sun was still shining. It was beaming hot as we walked down the steps of my house, but I was cool. Fact is, I felt like a celebrity on his way to the Oscars. Walking down the stairs, picnic basket in one hand, Brianna's hand in my other. She gave me the keys and I opened the passenger side door for her. I couldn't help but smile as I walked around to the driver's side. She opened my door from the inside. I slid into the all black leather interior with 5 on the floor (5 speed). I set the mirrors and turned the key. She had 'fortunate' by Maxwell in the CD player as I started the car. I looked at her and she looked at me. She placed her hand on top of mine as I shifted gears and pulled off. It must have taken me an hour to get to the end of my block. My house was on the third block in from the main intersection. That's how slow I was driving. I wanted EVERYONE on the block to see me and my Queen. We both had on shades and looked like Bobby & Whitney. OK, bad example, but we looked the part of a powerful, successful, and blessed to be together couple.

We finally made our way to the park and I parked under a tree in the shade. "Here sweetie, come and help me get this stuff out of the trunk." She took the basket and I grabbed the blanket, pillows, the game and a portable CD Player. We found a nice spot under a tree and she took the blanket from me and spread it out on the grass. "Here, come sit down with me." She took my hand and pulled me down next to her, then she laid back and kicked off her sandals. I sat up against the tree, took the pillow and laid it on my lap. She gently laid her head on the pillow face up, staring at me as I melted into her eyes. I begin to outline her eyebrows with my finger, and gently rub her bottom lip with my thumb.

"This feels soooo good!" she said. "Thank-you" "Thank me?" I asked "for what?" "For being such a nice guy! You really are a gentleman." "So tell me" she says, "tell me about Jay. I want to know all about Jay!"
again I drifted....

Where did you come from?....
Like a 'whisper'—you came into my life, gently whispering in my ear...that you are here
At a time when I needed you the most...when I needed love the most
When everywhere I turned, dark alleys appeared
Unable to understand why not a prayer did God hear
Trying my best to have the patience of Job...
Some nights I would get in the car and just drive...pull to the side, look to the sky and just cry
But I knew he was with me-he's covered me so many times....

I was just so tired...tired of playing this game we call love
Hopes and dreams dashed thru the arguments and screams
Who's there to hug a man when he needs to understand?
Everyone's threshold of pain is not the same, what one sees as sun the next may see as rain

Being approached by many not really wanting to deal with any
Why should I trust again? Why should I believe in her?
Just another form of the devil in disguise, I began to despise what I saw thru my own eyes
Not being able to trust enough in my heart to make a new start
Didn't want to face the pain of just falling apart...once again

And then came you…
It's been so long since I've believed in some one, some thing (other than the all mighty) as much as I believe in you. I've been waiting for you for so long. Never have I been so sure about any one thing in my life.
I've been waiting for you for so long! Where have you been?
That night…. I needed you…going to that place I called home, right into a violent argument—being accused up and down of infidelity, lies and betrayal
Checking my clothes for a certain fragrance, a certain smell…
I called for you….
Driving back from the game, me and the boys…laughing, just kickin it, making all kinds of noise
I got the call that my clothes were in the street because I was out with a woman accused of begin a liar and a cheat….
I cried for you…
The time I was awaken 3:00 in the morning—only to argue fuss and fight till the sun began dawning not able to function at work due to lack of sleep, migraine pounding. What would it be murder or suicide—had to be one or the other because I can't take it anymore….
It was then I prayed for you….

God has answered my prayers….
With the wind beneath your wings you have come as my Angel.
Unsure of how to deal with life's uncertainties, like a sudden breeze you have put my mind at ease
Please excuse me on certain days when I can't help but be amazed and with the woman that God has placed in my life

I promise to love you from the last strand on the top of your hair to the very tip of your longest toenail, and all that encompasses you as a woman, as who you are.

Don't get me wrong, sometimes I still find myself asking God "where did she come from"?
You are a blessing and I don't care where you came from or how you came, you're here and I know our lives will never be the same....

Chapter 3

Jayson McCallister

"Jay was a complicated guy. After being raised in a household of older siblings, it was no wonder early on I went in the direction I did. I was the youngest of four, by 10 years. I have 2 older brothers, and an older sister, Patricia. She's the oldest of us four. We called her Pat for short and she's 42. My brothers Ron & Mark are 41 and 40 with Ron being the older of the two.

Back in the day, hip-hop was just becoming main stream. Run-DMC, Kurtis Blow and the Sugar Hill gang. I loved 'em all. That's all I heard. Pat was into Tina Marie, Anita Baker, Phyllis Hyman. She was more reserved. Being 10 years younger I basically got what I wanted. Yeah, spoiled is a good word. My parents were older and didn't have the energy to keep up with me. Sure, they attended a few of my little league baseball and Pop Warner football games, but it was mainly my uncles who took interest. My fathers' brothers. When it came to discipline, my mom would be too tired from working two jobs and my father, who was a drummer in a Jazz band and was never home, would rarely discipline us. My mom would put the belt to us every now and then, but my father never, ever laid a finger on either of us. Like I said, when it came to laying the law, it was my uncles.

I saw a lot of what I now know as dysfunction. At that time, it was just life in the projects. My mom and dad would always fight over my dads' extra curricular activities. He would often physically abuse her, although mentally it was an everyday thing. He was not a provider, not in the least. Every year or so we were on the move but always within the same city.

I was very smart as a child, maybe too smart! I would always find a way to get what I needed. If I needed 100 penny candies for elementary school that day, then a few dollars would come up missing from SOMEONE in the house. I wouldn't graduate to stealing from outsiders until later on. Regardless of what was going on, we were always in church every Sunday, my mom and I. Ron, Mark and Pat were given options whether they wanted to go or not, not me. Ron and Mark were into sports and girls. They ran track together for their high school track team and both ended up going to Grambling University. They both ended up getting married early on also and both had four children. Pat was the smartest but she did not go to college. She had gotten pregnant at 18 and while her boyfriend, who was really a good guy and had planned on proposing to her when he came home from college for the baby's birth, was tragically killed in a car accident while on the way home when he got the word that my sister had went into labor. He was pronounced dead on the day my niece was born. Since then, her luck in men has gone downhill.

Even though we all loved each other, we never outwardly showed that type of affection. To this day we don't, but we know that we love each other.

At age 12, I began hanging out with older teens, most of which were already out of school. They took to me because I was good in sports. Basketball, football and baseball were my favorite sports, and I played all three equally well. With no one left at home but me, I had a lot of freedom…a lot of room for error. Age 13 is when I discovered sex and drugs.

I remember the first time I had an orgasm. I swore I had VD! I went around the school telling all my boys that this older girl gave me VD! They could care less about the VD but the fact that I had sex with a senior really put me on the map as far as status! Boy did I feel stupid when my older friends told me that it wasn't VD it was an orgasm, and that every time I had sex, that would happen. Again, I didn't have anyone to talk to me about these things, so I just went with whatever was told to me.

It was then that I started hanging out with Tracy Mackenzie and Curtis Wilson. We were in the same 6th grade class a year earlier. I had always known T-mac and Curt, but we really didn't start hangin' out until the 6th grade. That school year, my dad brought me one pair of pants, one shirt and a pair of converses for the new school year. He promised to get me more as the school year went on, but of course, he never did. My mom managed to get me a few more things as the year went on, but I was still far behind in the area of fashion. I would come home from school do my homework, and be out for most of the night, on a school night! Don't get me wrong, we would only be out in the courtyard, but it could be 12-1am before I came in. Drinking 40 ounces, smoking weed, going to the all night corner store when we had the munchies, really seemed like fun back then.

By the time I turned 14, the older guys would give me money to stay on the straight and narrow. Being that I was really good in sports and had played for the varsity high school teams while only in the 8th grade, I decided to leave the weed, drinking, and even the girls alone. I wanted to focus on athletics and hopefully get a scholarship to attend college. I was THAT good!

During the second half of my 8th grade year, right in the middle of football season, my mom informed me that we had to move. I was OK with that, even used to it, but this time to one city north of us to Linden, who was an arch rival of ours! I would also have to change schools! I couldn't believe it! I did not want any part of it, but if I wanted a place to sleep and eat, then

I had no choice. We moved. The only good thing about moving to Linden was the popularity factor. Guys from Linden.... I wouldn't say they were AFRAID of guys from Elizabeth, but they were AWARE of us! We had a reputation of fighting, and Linden was a suburb, a much quieter place, not as urban of a city like Elizabeth. It was definitely a step up from the projects. We moved to a two family house in a quiet neighborhood and life was supposed to get better for us. That's when things went downhill for ME!

Of course, I was NOT going to play for their sports teams, although I decided to play football the following season, but it just wasn't the same. That's when I met Darryl and Renardo, my other best friend. Renardo would die a few years later from what was said to be a drug overdose, but he was even sillier than Darryl. Before long, the rebellious stage set in and I did not want to go to school anymore. As soon as 10th grade hit, it was all about being cool and girls! Linden girls loved Elizabeth guys, and no guy in Linden had the heart to step to me because they knew where I was from and they did not want those type of problems, so I quickly became 'the man'. Like I said, I played football and my grades were always above average, but I HATED being there! I would always find some little chick with a crush on me to play hooky with me, all day long, at my house.

My mother and father left for work early and left me to go to school alone. BIG MISTAKE! We didn't get calls home to parents in Linden, just your occasional truant officer who was easy to get around. Renardo would take my room and I would take my moms room. Her and my dad had separate bedrooms, and hers was always clean. We would watch the soap operas from noon until 2:30 everyday, then walk up to the school to see who we could find to bring back to the house with us. My mom didn't get home until after 6. I made it through two years that way before I decided I wanted to quit in my last year, and that's what I did. I just had to talk my mom into it. I was too smart, they weren't teaching me anything I didn't already know. I wanted to buy this car I had my eye on, and I needed to *work to do that. These were my arguments to my mom and she went for it. I promised her I would get my G.E.D. and she OK'd my decision. I did what I set out to do. It took me a month and a half to get my G.E.D. from an adult learning center. After that, I got a job in the factory that my mom worked making $4.25 an hour driving a forklift. I was able to save up and get my car. Boy was I on top of the world!*

I had a girlfriend by this time…a steady girlfriend named Miriam. Miriam came to live with us while she was still a sophomore in high school. She had family issues as well, much deeper than mine. She had 4 brothers and 3 sisters all living in a two bedroom house and her father was still out there creating new life. He would cruise the high schools in the area finding gullible young girls to entrust him by offering them rides and buying them ice cream and such. Then he would hit on them. Hell, some of them were even Miriam's classmates. She became pregnant and after she had my son Justin, we moved into our first apartment, which was where else but back in Elizabeth. This was the beginning of my end.

Only making enough to take care of me while living at home, money became an issue. Now I had rent, bills, car insurance, baby, girlfriend…all my responsibility. Miriam wasn't working, hell she was still in school. I would still hang out with Darryl and Renardo however, this wasn't making it. I couldn't survive like this. My mom told me before I moved out, that coming back home wouldn't be an option. This is the life I wanted, so this is the life I had to deal with. I would go hang out back in the projects I came from, the buildings that raised me. After work, that was my first and sometimes last stop for the night. I usually had a girl with me. Don't get me wrong, I cared for Miriam, but I was young and very irresponsible at that time. I was not ready for the path God was taking me down. I was never the type to sleep around…I was too afraid of diseases, but I would always love to meet a pretty young thang and get her to fall in love with me. I would parade her around in front of the felllas then dump her when the next pretty face came along. That's how my reputation grew as a 'playa'.

Having them fight over me, having jealous boyfriends try to find out who I was, them buying me things and giving me money all was good enough. I didn't NEED to sleep with them. I had a girlfriend at home for that. Before long, smokin' weed and drinking 40's became a regular thing again.

I hadn't been in Elizabeth that much since we moved to realize that a whole new epidemic was sweeping the neighborhood and very soon sweeping the county, and the nation. Crack! We didn't know about crack in Linden, but when Miriam and I moved back to Elizabeth and I began hanging out again, oh, stuff had changed! The older guys I used to hang with were now selling rock and making a killing! I wanted a piece of that quick, easy money. The police weren't even that bad at that time. Once I began selling crack, money was no issue. I would be out 2-3 days at a time, up for 24 hours a day. It was a full time job, serving crack fiends. Bills were paid, I had a nice car, and I brought Miriam a little car to get back and forth to nursing school. We moved to a better place. Yeah, things were great!

Miriam became pregnant with my daughter Kaley. We were living well, eating well, and OK with life. I still had my women on the side which might cause an occasional argument, but she really had no clue. All she knew is that I was making money. I would even take her with me sometime to N.Y. to pick up a new package of drugs to sell. Like I said, things were fine. That would change on one of my usual trips to N.Y. to pick-up. The Colombian that I would buy from, who sold me crack, asked me if I ever sold straight Cocaine. He said it would sell just as fast as the crack because a lot of fiends preferred to 'cook-up' their coke to form crack. It was supposed to be a 'better type' of crack. I told him I had heard about it, but never sold it. He gave me an 8-ball and told me to sell it. An 8-ball was an 8th of an ounce of cocaine. He even laid some out on the table and told me to try it. Not wanting to seem corny or worse yet, like the Feds (by not trying a drug in front of them might seem suspicious to some dealers), I tried it. He laid out a few lines and he sniffed them first. Then he laid out a few

for me and I sniffed them. This was the first time I had EVER put anything up my nose but nasal spray. It felt good. I liked the high. It was intense. I did manage to sell some, but I soon became dependant of it. I wanted it, and I needed it daily. It began to control me. This is how the progression went, and in no time at all;
Buying coke-selling coke
Buying coke-selling 'some' coke
Buying coke-snorting coke-not selling coke
Stealing to buy coke

Just that quick it had me! I became broke, and began stealing to support my new habit. It became progressively worse. After stealing items out of my own house to sell, basically for nothing, Miriam couldn't take it anymore. Rent was 3 months past due, utilities were off and no food was in the house. I didn't care, I was never there anyway. When she took the kids and moved in with one of her sisters, I couldn't understand why! What was wrong with HER? She never looked back.

It took a lot for me to succumb to the fact that I had become the people I would sell crack to…a fiend! I was a drug addict, addicted to cocaine. Then came the gun stage. I would carry a pistol and I would go on to rob drug dealers, steal stashes or whatever it took to get that next high. I had become a hardened criminal in no time at all. I knew it had gotten bad when I stole from my mom.
I also took from my family and people who used to trust me.

It didn't matter. Before long, people would hate to see me coming. One night, my first cousin, my uncles son who was a pretty big drug dealer in midtown, had a pistol put to his head by me, his blood. He had decided he wasn't going to give me anymore cocaine because I was killing myself, so I took it! His last words to me were…."someone is going to kill you Jay, but it won't be me!" He was killed about 6 months later by some girl's jealous boyfriend. He was right, someone WAS going to kill me, eventually, but I didn't care at that time.

Finally, one night after being up for about 5 days straight, I couldn't get any higher than I was. I just wanted it to stop! I was hiding out over someone's house that I didn't even know! All I know is that he got high too. I had to do something! I couldn't take it anymore! Like my cousin said, someone was going to kill me or either I would O.D. Either way, I just wanted it to stop. That night I formulated a plan. The next morning, I would go to Broad St., which was the main shopping district of the city, and I would rob the McDonald's restaurant when it opened, get on the train to N.Y., get high, come back and turn myself into the police. That's how bad I wanted the madness to stop!

After spending that night looking out the window for my next victim, the next morning came. I had two pistols tucked under my shirt and I was off to Broad St. around 5:30am. McDonald's opened at 6 and I could catch the manager as he was going in. By the time I got to Broad St., the morning commuters were on their way to work on this busy street. I hadn't eaten in days. My stomach was hurting, felt like my ribs were touching. I weighed about a buck forty, had a nappy beard and the curls in my head were untamed. I looked a hot mess!, at least that's what I was told by this young lady that I had known and had asked for a dollar to get a donut from the donut shop next to McDonald's. They had just put out some fresh morning donuts and I was starving. "Hey Tina, can I borrow a dollar," I said. "I don't have a dollar...wait a minute...is that YOU Jay?" "Yeah its me, oh now you don't know me?" "You look a hot mess...look at you! get away from me!" and she hurried away from me. "What was wrong with HER" I asked myself again.

See, everyone else had the problem, not me! Not even thinking about WHY she reacted that way. That's OK, a few more minutes and it'll be on anyway.

Broad Street was lined with stores all up and down. Clothing stores, department stores, shoe stores, nail salons…everything. I went and stood in the doorway to a clothing store next to McDonald's as I waited for the manager to open. The store had a full length mirror inside the store facing the window. While standing there, I happened to glance at that mirror and actually see myself for the first time in over a month. I couldn't believe it! I touched my face and felt all the hair. I pulled together my shirt and pulled up my sagging pants. At that time, all I could do is drop to my knees. What had I become?! It was then I called for Jesus! I cried and I cried. I cried like a baby for about 20 minutes, I mean boo-hooing. People were walking by on their way to work, some standing there waiting for the bus…. I didn't care. I had to allow him in! Funny, but not one person asked if I was OK or if I needed help. I picked myself up, dried my face with my shirt, looked up and told Jesus "Thank you!"

I went into that McDonalds, which was open now, and instead of robbing him, I asked to use the restroom. I took the clips from out of the guns, and wrapped them in a napkin and put them in my pocket. I wrapped up the guns too, and put them in a plastic bag that was in the bathroom. I picked up the bag and was on my way out when the manager stopped me and asked me if I would like some hotcakes and orange juice. Wow! And this is a man that I could have possibly killed had he been 30 minutes early for work that day! A big smile came over my face. I knew then that God had me! After I ate, I thanked the manager and went and threw the bag in the garbage. Then I threw the clips in the sewer and flagged down a police car. There were two officers inside and I told them I had a drug problem and that I needed help. After twenty minutes of calling around on their radios, they found the only detox in the area with an available bed but it was two cities away. I was so upset I almost cried. I didn't have bus fare to go that far. One of the officers saw my face and he talked the officer that was driving into taking me there. Wow! God at work again!

I realize now that God sends angels in many shapes and sizes, many colors with many different occupations. It was THAT day that taught me that!

I was in St. Judes hospital for 5 days before they told me my time had run out. They can only keep a person in detox for 5 days. They gave me the option of either going back home or I could go to a rehab for 28 days. Well, I didn't have insurance for the rehab and I didn't have a home to go to. Now what would I do? After having those 5 days to reflect—eat and sleep, I did not want to go back out onto those streets. I was terrified! Not of who was out there looking for me, but of that drug! I knew it was still out there, waiting for me! I got down on my knees that night, my last night there, and prayed for God to intervene. The next morning as I was getting my things together, the nurse from the unit came in and told me that she called the rehab that morning and that they would be willing to take me as a charity case! This was one of if not the best rehab in the state! She said I could go into the 28 day inpatient program they had and I would not have to pay a dime! Boy God was good! All I had to do was call his name.

The first thing I saw when I got to the rehab center, while waiting in the intake room was the poem 'footprints'....

I Had a Dream

> One night I had a dream
> I was walking along the beach with my Lord.
> Across the sky flashed scenes from my life.
> For each scene I noticed two sets
> of footprints in the sand,
> one belonging to me
> and the other to my Lord.
> When the last scene of my life shot before me
> I looked back at the footprints in the sand.

There was only on set of footprints.
I realized that this was at the lowest
and saddest times in my life.
This always bothered me
and I questioned the Lord
about my dilemma.
"Lord, you told me when I decided to follow You,
You would walk and talk with me all the way.
But I'm aware that during the most troublesome
times of my life there is only one set of footprints.
I don't understand why, when I needed you most,
you'd leave me."
He whispered, "My precious, precious child,
I love you and will never leave you
never, ever during your times of trial and testings.
When you saw only one set of footprints in the sand,
It was then that I carried you."

Margaret Fishback Powers
Footprints in the Sand

I cried like a baby after reading this…
I began to find out about this disease, about me. I wasn't the monster I thought I had become. I didn't come from the slum of the earth. I was not bad, hateful or mean. I wasn't a criminal. I didn't mean to rob, hurt and steal from people.… I was sick. The people in the rooms of AA and NA were my medicine. I had rediscovered God and I talked with him daily. When I left the rehab, I went to stay with my mom. Leaving rehab was one of the saddest times in my life. I was leaving a group of people who understood me…who were LIKE me! They were doctors, lawyers, nuns, priests, teachers, felons and judges but we were all the same there. There was no

one to judge me, no one to ridicule me, no one to be ashamed of. We all shared one common bond. We had a disease.

My mom was soooo happy when I came home. I immediately wanted to make amends, which was one of the 12 steps laid out in the program. I tried to call Mariam, but she still didn't want anything to do with me. She had moved on, and THIS time I understood why. I went to meetings everyday for the first two years of my recovery. I changed people, places, and things and began to set priorities in my life. Darryl had also gone through rehab, and he too was turning his life around. Through all the madness that I went thru, he was right there with me. We went thru it together, so he understood when I went into rehab. He checked in a week later. I got my first office job from speaking at an NA meeting one night. This guy who would later become my sponsor whom had 17 years of sobriety, would be the person who would teach me the in's and out's of the business world. He offered me a job telemarketing at his company that he owned, and paid me $7.00 an hour. Anyone who was not living their life clean, sober and for God, I did not associate myself with.

Big things have happened since then. That was 6 years ago and I am living a totally different life. I was always smart, so incorporating street skills into the corporate world was a natural fit for me. One good job led to another good job and God placed me in a position to be successful, to live life on its own terms. Those first two years out of rehab I didn't even date. I had to learn about Jay. What caused me to go off the deep end? Was it my upbringing? Was it that I was left to discover manhood on my own? Why did I misuse women, not allowing anyone to get close enough to really know me, the real me? Fact is, I didn't even know me, and I am still learning!

I'm not one to sit here and tell you that life is all good even now. I'm 30 years old and still don't know how to love, but I believe just like anything else, God will teach me the way to do that as well. He's brought me so far. People trust me again. I'm allowed at family functions now. I have a suc-

cessful career and I am a productive father to my children. The only thing missing is love. I've had relationships the past 3 years, but like I stated earlier, I would purposely sabotage them if I felt a woman getting too close. But I am ready now. I am ready to really, truly love. I am ready for the next chapter."

As the sky turned to dusk, I looked down at Brianna, she had tears in her eyes. "What's wrong baby?" I said. "I can't believe you've been thru all of that in your past" she said. "You are an amazing man Mr. McCallister and I feel special even having the chance to hear your story. That is quite a testimony you have," she continued. "What you don't know is that I can relate because I too had a brother. A brother who was caught up in the same things you were only he wasn't as fortunate." "What happened", I said. "He overdosed on heroin when I was a junior in college." "I'm so sorry" "Oh, it's OK now, I've healed." "It was tough convincing my mother that God needed him in heaven." "God kept you here Jay because you have more work to do here on earth."

Brianna was a Christian as well, which made it even sweeter. I'm far from perfect and I know I still have a long way to go, but today I know God. We're on a first name basis! Most of my prayers consist of giving thanks, rather than asking for things. He already knows what I need, but I ASKED him for Brianna. As she closed her eyes, I gently moved the pillow off of my lap and laid it beside me with her head still on it. I slid down next to her on the blanket. I watched her as she slept and I asked God to place in me the ability to love, honestly and openly. Without any restrictions, or reservations. Unconditionally, without looking for anything in return. I wanted her. I wanted us....

CHAPTER 4

▼

BRIANNA WILLIAMS

(Alarm clock goes off) "Man, is it 7:30 already?" Church services begin a 9:30 but I would always need a little extra time. I'd lie in the bed that beautiful Sunday morning thinking of Brianna. The blinds were open and the sun was creeping in. I had the windows open so that I can feel the early morning breeze. I wondered what she was doing. Was she still asleep? Had she already awaken? I wanted so bad to call her, but I didn't want her to think I was a stalker or maybe something worse, calling her so early in the morning. Brianna seemed to occupy my every thought. Every 30 seconds... is a new thought of her.
(Phone rings) "Good morning sleepy head, did I wake you?" "Hey Brianna, as a matter of fact, you didn't." "My alarm clock just went off 5 minutes ago and I was just lying here thinking." "Thinking about what?" "Thinking about this wonderful woman I just met." "Does this woman have a name?" "I think its Brianne, Briel...something like that." "I think you mean Brianna!" "Yeah, that's her name!" "Do you know her?" I said. "I heard some things about her." "She's OK." "Good choice if I must say so myself." We both start laughing. "Well, I beat you to it," she said. "I've been up since 6:30, and I've been thinking about you since 6:31." "I started to call you, but I didn't want you to think I was some crazed

women, calling you so early in the morning, so I got up—showered, did my hair and made me a little breakfast." "My church service begins at 9:00 and I was hoping I could speak to you a little before I left." "Thank you," I said. "For what?" she asked. "For allowing your voice to be the first sound I heard this morning, besides my alarm clock, but that doesn't count." "You are so sweet Jay!" "Shhhhhh, don't tell anyone, it might ruin my image!" "Are you dressed already?" I asked. "Not at all. I still have on my nighty." "Lucky nighty!" I thought to myself. "So who do you live with Bri?" "I live alone." "I had a roommate, but she never wanted to pay her half of the rent and utilities, so I kindly asked her to leave. It's been three months now that I've lived alone, and the truth is, I really like it this way." "If I want to walk around my house with nothing but my underwear, I can do that without having to worry whether or not she has a man in her room who just may see me if he came out." "She would always have SOMEONE spending the night." "That didn't bother you?" "Of course it did, but in her line of work…never mind, but YES, it bothered me." "I'm just happy she's gone." "So, what church do you attend?" she asked. "I am a member of New Order Christian Church. It's located in Edison, and you?" "I attend the Living Well Christian Center in New Brunswick." "I've been a member there for six years," she said. "Hey, I have an idea…why don't we visit each others church?" I asked. "Today we can go to mine, and next Sunday we can attend yours." "I would love to, what time does your service begin?" "9:30" I said. "Ok, you can pick me up at 9:00 if that's ok with you." "My address is 231 Warren St., 2nd fl." Brianna lived in Roselle, which was 10 minutes from me. "9:00 will be fine." "See you then." "Should I make you something to eat?" she asked. "No, that's ok, we can pick up something after service." "Ok, see you at 9 Jay." "Just ring the upstairs doorbell." "Ok baby, see you then."

Just the fact that she ASKED if I wanted her to make me something to eat made me feel like a million dollars! Wow, I am actually taking this woman to church with me! This is definitely a first!

I cannot believe I just met her two days ago, but I'm really feeling her. She seems to be a wonderful young lady. I wonder why she doesn't have a man. Can this be just a mirage? I was told that I am one who always sees the glass half-empty. If something is too good, there has to be a catch. Maybe Darryl, Curt and T. set me up! Maybe they PAID her to be nice to me for my birthday weekend and then come Monday…WHAM!! It would be all over with. I could picture their faces laughing at me now!
(Phone rings) "Hello"…. "What's up J-smooth?" It was Darryl. "Yo, did you, Curt and T. pay Brianna to be nice to me for my birthday weekend?" I asked. "Man, how did you find out?" "I knew it!" "You know what D, don't even call my house anymore!" "I gotta go. I'm about to call her and give Ms. Christian lady a piece of my mind." "ahahahahahah…naw man, no one paid her to be nice to you fool!" "What are you smoking over there?" he said laughing. He continued, "Oh, I see—here we go again. Looking for reasons already huh?" "What's wrong now Jay?" "Is she TOO beautiful?" "Please man, you know that's my style," I said. "Then what is it?" "Is she too sweet? Too smart? Does she make too much money? Is her car not new enough? Which excuse is it THIS time?" "Whatever man, I just asked a question." "Yeah, we really need to meet today," Darryl said. "You need a word!" "Oh yeah, the meeting," I said. "Tell Curt and T. that it is going to have to be around 5 or 6 tonight, cool?" "Why? Church is over at 12 my brother," he asked. "Bri is going to church with me and we'll probably stop at Ray-Ray's to get something to eat afterwards." "Get something to eat?!" "You really like this girl huh? Taking her to church with you?!" "I hope you know that walking into God's house with a woman on your arm is serious business." "It's like taking her to meet your mom. Those are two things you just can't play around with." "Louise (Darryl's mom) don't play that. I'd better have an engagement ring in my pocket if I plan on walking through HER door with a woman or she won't even ask the girl to sit down. She's from the old school and Jesus has been around longer than she has, so I really hope your intentions are for real here fella!" "Don't worry about me partner. What's up with Karen? Did she give in yet?" I asked. "Naw man, Karen is like a leopard, she wants to be hunted." "I am going to take one

more shot and if I miss again, I'm out of that forest!" "I hear that," I said. "Don't forget to let Curt and T. know that 6:00 would be a real good time for me. I will get with you guys then." "Peace" "Peace"

Man, Bri lives on a really nice block! She MUST have money! Even to rent an apartment here has to be expensive! Her house was beautiful with neatly trimmed manicured grass and hedges. It wasn't as pretty as her, but not much was.
(doorbell rings) "Hold on one second Jay!" "Here, take the keys and let yourself in." She dropped the keys from her bedroom window. I opened the front door and walked up the stairs to the door at the top of the stairs. "Man, I hope this girl don't have a messy house." That was a pet peeve of mine. As I stated earlier, I hate a mess. I walked in and all I saw was crystal everywhere, beautiful paintings, and very decorative euro-centric furniture. "Wow!" "What type of business are you in again and are they hiring?!" I shouted out to her. "You are so silly!" "I see why you and Darryl are best friends. Have a seat and I will be right out. If you would like something to drink, help yourself. I have juice in the fridge." On her mantle, I see pictures…a lot of pictures. In these pictures, and there had to be maybe 25-30 pictures which were all in frames, there was Brianna and various females. Not one picture had a man in it. I am trying my best not to think anything negative, so I'm going to let these thoughts go. She just has a lot of friends that's all! Hmmmmmm. "I'll be out in a second sweetie." "Take your time, I'm enjoying your furniture." "Hey, watch it! It's not that type of furniture!" Bri had a sense of humor too and that was a beautiful thing. One thing a man hates is to have a woman who is a prude, you know. Dull, boring, never smiles or laughs. Basically just doesn't know how to have fun. That definitely wasn't Brianna. "How do I look?" She came out from the back room in this really, really gorgeous black and white dress that wasn't too tight and wasn't too loose. She had on a pair of funky black and white shoes with three inch heals. Yeah, she was wearin' it well! "Um, um, um…how do you look?" I asked. "Blessed!" She flashed that gorgeous smile of hers. "Ready to go?" I asked. "Let me get my purse and we'll be on our

way, unless you got me on the collection plate!" she joked. "And you say I'M silly!" As we drove down the highway in my Cadillac Northstar, I had on BeBe Winans' "Dream" cd. The song "Help is on the way" was playing. I always listen to Gospel music on Sunday Morning. "Brianna, let me ask you a question, why was a beautiful woman like you alone?" (Notice I said was) She glanced out of the passenger side window for a second and then turned to me. "Because men don't understand me," she said. "Please elaborate"

"I am a down to earth woman, with values. A woman who wants the best that life can offer me. I learned a long time ago, while I was still in high school, that when men see me, they see beauty and that's it. Their thoughts of what a relationship should be become distorted. They want to control me. They want to tell me when and where to go and what time to be back. I have yet to meet a man who was not afraid to let me be me. I too am the youngest of my siblings. I have an older sister and then there was my brother that passed. My mom taught me how to be a woman, a woman like her. She taught me what to expect and what not to expect from a man. Grown men were trying to hit on me ever since I was in the 8th grade. Once I reached adulthood, I had to learn what was real and what was fake. When my brother passed I could not function for a while because he was the closest one to me. He knew me, he understood me and before the drugs took over, he was a father to me. My father died of cancer when I was 13 and my mom chose to raise her children instead of searching for another man. She was strong, but she only saw things from a woman's eyes. That's why my brother had such an impact on me. When he succumbed to the life of drugs, a part of me went with him. After that, I had only my mother's wisdom to follow. She taught me how to be independent, to not have to wait nor depend on a man, how to make MYSELF happy. That way of thinking did not sit well in a few of the relationships I had. Some men are intimidated by a woman that controls her own destiny. I'm strong, beautiful, and self-sufficient and not trying to play these games men play, but to be honest with you Jay, I'm tired of being this way.

I really wish there WAS a man I could trust enough to let my guard down and be who I really want to be. Understand this, I know the way my mother raised me is not the way God intended for a woman to be, and I do know that the women that ARE this way were more than likely FORCED into this role by a man who couldn't hold his own. I wasn't forced to be this way, I was taught. I WANT to love, openly and honestly. I WANT to have a man that I can depend on, a man who would show me the true meaning of love. A man of God."

I could tell she was sincere. She looked at me again and she had tears in her eyes. I took the next exit off the expressway and pulled over to the side of the road. With my thumb, I gently wiped away a tear that had fallen down her cheek. "God gives us blessings to see if we can handle them," I said. We have to recognize those blessings for what they are when they are given." "Those who don't know the Lord will look those blessings right in the face and not even realize what they are, then it's gone. She leaned over and gently kissed my lips. "Are you my blessing Jay?" "That's a question only God himself can answer," I said. We kissed again—It was a precious moment.

On my forehead I catch a drop of rain…starts at the top of my head and runs down my vein
A subtle glimpse at you—is all I need, not a stare….
but you look so good, that it's just not fair
A walk in the park as the sky gets dark your arms around my waist as passing dogs bark
Let's go for a ride…lay your hand on my thigh, your head on my shoulder…stare at the sky as I drive
The circular motion of a lathered sponge on your chest, as I bathe you in hot water…you lay back to relieve the stress
Lie your head on my lap as I read you a book, my arms around your waist as you try to cook…

Precious Moments….

The first sign of snow, locked in and all
no mall for you, for me no ball
let's see a show tonight, maybe the Whispers…aaiiiight!!
then we'll stroll on the boardwalk, stealing kisses under the lights
A power outage, we can't find our clothes
but heck who needs em', in the dark…anything goes
Taking cruises, watching muses lighting fuses on the 4th of July,
on the sofa watching Cooley High trying to be a man, but can't
help but cry

Precious Moments…

Let me massage your toes, let's go nose to nose—it's Sunday night
and we're wishing time froze
At Christmas time we're under the mistletoe, who needs a gift
how 'bout you in a bow
In the delivery room, the pain is great
but for our bundle of joy, it will be well worth the wait
In 20 years I will still visualize
the precious moments we've shared and will share
for the rest of our lives!

Many Precious Moments

Chapter 5

▼

The meeting

Church service was really good that day and rather prophetic if I may say so myself. Our pastor was at another church this particular Sunday as a guest Pastor, so our Junior Pastor gave the sermon for the day. The reason I said it was prophetic was because his sermon was on love, relationships, marriage, the woman's role in a marriage and how many men today fall short of establishing the foundation, the base of what a Christian home should be. This was coming from a man 6 years younger than me. It's amazing when I think about it. At his age, I was on a downward spiral, yet this young man could stand before a church of over 1800 members not counting guests and deliver a word that men twice—heck three times his age knew nothing about. Brianna really enjoyed the service and even said she wanted to go again.

After church we stopped by Ray-Ray's, and had breakfast. Yeah, she got to see me grub, after which I dropped her off at home. "Am I going to see you tonight?" I asked. "I'm sorry baby, but I have to work tonight, but I would love to see you one day this week if you're not busy." 'Cool" I said. I wonder what type of job you can have that you have to work Sunday night, unless you're either a cop, work in a hospital, or a security guard!? "But I can call you later on," she said. *"Ok"* She leaned over and gave me a nice, sweet, soft kiss. All of a sudden I forgot about her job.

Later on early that evening, I met the fellas for our meeting.
"Man, you BETTER had made it tonight. One more excuse and you would have been voted O-U-T partner!"
Curt was a rather dramatic type of guy—always talked with his hands, a lot of motion with not a whole lot to say. We met over Darryl's house. It would either be my place or D's because we were the one's that didn't have a woman around. *"So what's up fellas?"* I asked. *"We know what's up with YOU,"* Curt said. *"Man, give a brother a break"* T. chipped in. *"Jay just wants the same thing we all want…a good woman."* *"How many good women has Jay had?"* said Darryl *"All he's gonna do is find another reason to not want her and Brianna will be gone just like the rest."* *"Look who thinks they have this thing figured out,"* I said making reference to Darryl. *"When was the last time YOU had a girl that you didn't need to wait for visitation day to go see?"* *"You've been to more prisons than Mike Tyson and to more rehabs that Bobby Brown and that was to visit your girl-friends!"* *"I just make bad choices in women, that's all."* *"Yeah, I would say 3 to 5 was a bad choice!"* 3 to 5 was the nickname of one of Darryl's girls. We gave her that name because she was out on parole from serving a 3 to 5 year prison term for aggravated assault on one of her ex boyfriends. *"Man, forget that, Barbara is driving me CRAZY!"* said Curt. Barbara was his girl, his baby's momma. *"Why don't you just marry her and get it over with man?"* Darryl asked. *"Why would I want to get married now?"* *"That would just complicate things."* *"Face it Curt, the only one complicated in your relationship is you,"* I said. See, men don't have a problem telling another man just how it is. We usually call it like we see it. I don't know how women do it, but men generally don't cut corners. *"Barbara is a really nice girl. Personally, I think it's just HER you don't want to marry."* I said. *"Let me ask you, are you saying you will NEVER get married, to Barbara or anyone else?"* I asked. *"I'm not saying that, but Barbara and I argue too much."* *"Really?"* Darryl stepped in. *"Think it has anything to do*

with…ummmmm, let me see…her car getting keyed up? or what was it, her tires being flattened or wow, what was that other thing…oh yeah, females calling your house telling her they were with you the night before? Oh yeah, it was one more thing,…" "man, why the heck would you give some woman your home number anyway?" T-mac asked. "I've been meaning to ask you that." Curt starts with the hand motions, "naw man, see she was a co-worker right, and she needed a ride to work the next day right, and I gave her my number and told her to call me in the morning when she was ready and I would be by to pick her up on my way in. I just happened to not be able to pick her up one morning, and she tried to get back at me, that's all." "Curt, she dropped your draws off and hung them from Barbara's car antenna man," Darryl said. "Did you sleep with her Curt?" I asked. "Yeah, but what does that…" "See, my point exactly!" I said. "YOU are the one who complicates things." "I just don't know how she puts up with your behind and for as long as she has," said T. "and she stays faithful to this fool!"

"See, me and Blink got plans!" "I realize what I have." "She may not be the prettiest, the best cook, or have the greatest body, but I know her heart." T. said. "We're friends before anything else." "I trust her and she knows I would never do anything to hurt her. My frat boys can't understand that, and when we're out they always try to get me to push up on some shortie, but that's not my style." "I would never do anything to her that I would not want her to do to me while she is out with her friends. We don't have issues like that." "So, when are you guys takin' it to the end zone?" (getting married) I asked. "I don't know man, but I'm gonna propose to her real soon! I have to before someone else snatches her up." "So, tell us about Brianna Jay," T. said. "Brianna is BAD!" said Darryl. "I really don't know a whole lot about her yet, but she seems like a remarkable woman. She and I went to my church this morning. She lives in Roselle in this really nice two family house. She's in the entertainment industry. I believe a manager or something like that. As a matter of fact, she had to work tonight." I said. "Working on a Sunday night?" asked D. "You better check that out!" "Does she manage singers, music groups, comedians…what?" said Curt. "I really don't know, but she has a gang of girlfriends. That I know. All over her house she's in pictures with different females." "REALLY!" said Curt. "Hook a brother up!" "Man, you better worry about Barbara and leave the playin to the playa's" I said. "You're washed up," Darryl said talking to Curt. "Your playa card is in review and about to be snatched! Women calling your house!?" We all started laughing. "So are you going to really give you and Brianna a shot Jay?" asked T. "Yeah, I believe so T., but I'll be honest with you, it's something about giving my heart to a woman that scares me. As much as I want to fall in love, it's really hard for me to just let go. Women don't understand that. They think just because we are men, we don't have a heart. It should be no problem just falling in love because we're not going to give as much as them emotionally in the relationship anyway, but women are emotional creatures by nature, so it's easier for them to just give their hearts and fall in love. With men, it's a struggle between our minds and our male ego. Once we can convince our mind that it's cool and can hold off our ego until our heart takes over, then we got it." "I will tell you this though, if it's going to happen, Brianna is the type of woman I would definitely want it to happen with." "aaaawww-www…Jay's in love!" "Be quiet Curt," I said. "That's something YOU should've been in the past 15 years." "I was…for the first two maybe three." "What is it now Curt?" T-mac asked. "I'm in LIKE!" Again, we busted out laughing. "You've got serious issues my brother," said D. "Look who's talking about issues." "A man who dated a woman with six kids by five different dudes for three days and the following week thought he was the father of her seventh just because she told him she was pregnant again!" Curt said. "If you recall, that little episode got YOUR playa card REVOKED!" At that point we were on the floor crying we were laughing so hard! "I don't know what's so funny, I was just being responsible." "You were just being STUPID!" I said. "Now why do I have to be stupid Jay?" "Obviously, for you to think that you had a shot at being daddy number seven, you had to sleep with her within those first three days of meeting her

AND without a condom! What do YOU call it?" "HORNY!" said T. Again, we were on the floor rollin'! Even Darryl had to laugh this time. (Phone rings) "Hello" said Darryl. "Hey Darryl, can I speak to Curtis please, this is Barbara." "Hey Barbara, what's up girl? Curt isn't here! Did he tell you he was coming here again? I am so sick of that boy using me to sneak out and do whatever it is he has to do, but I know where he is, do you want me to see if I can reach him for you?" "Give me the phone stupid! You play too much!" "Man, I'm getting ready to go," I said. "I gotta go home and do a few things to get ready for work tomorrow." Really, I just wanted to be home in case Brianna called. "Next week fellas?" I asked. "Fo sho," said T. "Tell ya girl I said waaaaaazzzzuuupppp!" "D, I'll get at you later on tonight." "Peace." "Peace."

Chapter 6

▼

I'm Falling!

By the time I got home, I was drained. Up early in the morning, being intoxicated with Brianna earlier today and dealing with my boys this evening, had me mentally, emotionally and physically drained. The time was 8:45pm and I really didn't have anything to do but relax and ready myself mentally for work the next day. On Friday I would begin to mentally prepare myself for the weekend, and Sunday night it would be mental preparations for Monday. I really didn't want to do anything either, but write. Oh yeah, did I mention I was a writer? I used to rap when I was younger, but I never really went anywhere with it. Everyone locally knew I had skills, but as I mentioned in an earlier chapter, I had other priorities other than chasing a dream. I eventually turned to poetry. It really became prevalent while I was in rehab. I would write at night while I was there, and would then recite during our daily meetings. I would write for those that needed it, and it would be a big help to a lot of my peers in rehab. The day I left, so many people cried and told me how much I had been an inspiration to them thru my words. Mostly everyone who signed my AA and NA books that day all had something to say about my poetry...
"Jay, my brother...you are truly blessed. I have truly enjoyed my time here with you and I know you are going to make it when you hit the

bricks. You have been an inspiration to us all with your poetry. Never stop writing and remember to keep God first in your life. It works if you work it." Signed Rev. George Peeples.

There were many, many more inscriptions like that. A few people even said that I would end up in the pulpit, Pastor of my own church! God hasn't called me there yet, but I still write, especially when I have something to motivate me to do so. Brianna was my motivation. Every time I think of her, I get this warm fuzzy feeling all over…A tingle. No other woman has affected me this way. I did not want to force myself to believe I was falling in love with this woman, after all, we had just met and I was not one to believe in love at first sight. I felt love had to be earned. Love took time and anyone who could fall in love with someone they just met was simply being foolish, so I thought.

In the past, it would be very easy for me to tell a woman I loved her at the drop of a hat, but those were just words. I could've told a monkey and the meaning would've been the same as me telling a female. I just refused to allow myself to get that far into anyone. Now I have all these feelings that I am trying to deal with, rationally. Can you rationalize love? I truly don't know the answer to that. All I know is that I am feeling some sorta way about Bri. One thing anyone who knows me can tell you about me is that I am passionate. Passion is something I was born with. I just needed to realize that there are things that are WORTH being passionate about. Then there are times when the things I was passionate about were the wrong things. So the goal is not to CONTROL my passion, but to channel it in the right direction. I think passion is the most underrated emotion God has given us and definitely the most misused. If you can think of all the things that people are passionate about, better yet, take people you know. Just thinking about it—my mom is passionate about playing the lottery, Darryl is passionate about Playstation, T. is passionate about his car but what does it all mean? Allow me break it down;

Passion...

As describe in the dictionary;
(2) plural : the emotions as distinguished from reason b : intense, driving, or overmastering feeling or conviction.
5 a : ardent affection : LOVE b : a strong liking or desire for or devotion to some activity, object, or concept c : sexual desire d : an object of desire or deep interest
synonym—PASSION, FERVOR, ARDOR, ENTHUSIASM, ZEAL mean intense emotion
compelling action. PASSION applies to an emotion that is deeply stirring or ungovernable <was a slave to his passions>.

As described by me;
Passion is what one feels first within himself before it can be displayed to others....
Passion is what one feels within his soul. Standing up, professing feelings that others cannot and never will not, understand.

Passion gives you the freedom to express your desires...experiencing life's emotions whether positive or negative.
You no longer have to be curled up like a ball; afraid to release for fear of being hurt once again.... Passion sets you free within yourself.

Seeking the strength and the energy to face rational or irrational thoughts, with a mind tarnished by jealousy, envy and sometime pure hatred for those that dare to compare me with an ordinary man...searching for a power that only God can instill with his graces and his will...Passion gives you the strength to seek that power.

My reason for being blessed with breath is my Passion for life...

For fear that I could have been born Passionless, never knowing the meaning of certain feelings, certain experiences would have came and went without even a hint of what it was all about…what it all meant.

My Passion drives me to be the best man I can be…the best father I can be…the best son, and the best brother I can be.
One day my Passion will overflow to the one I love and allow me to be the best husband I can be….

And only then…

Will a lifetime be formed.

(Phone rings) "Hello" "Hey sweetie, sounds like I woke you." It was Brianna. "What time is it?" I asked half out of my mind. "It's 12:45 baby. I am so sorry for calling you so late, but I did tell you that I would call you and I wanted to keep my word." "Besides, I've been thinking about you all night!" "Isn't that sweet, but where are you hon? I can barely hear you!" "Oh, I'm still working. I should be done in an hour or so," she said. "Sounds like you're at a club!" I said. "I did tell you I'm in the entertainment industry sweetie. It's all work, trust me. I'm not here because I wanna be," "Is someone performing?" I asked. "Something like that," she replied. "I just wanted to tell you goodnight love and sweet dreams, but only if they're of me! I'll call you tomorrow." "Ok, talk to you then," I said.

*"Boy, why can't **I** have a job like that," I thought to myself. Hangin' out, partying AND getting paid for it! My job was not as glamorous. I had a basic 9-6 with benefits and free internet service. The most exciting thing about my job was discovering a new computer virus. I think it was really sweet of her to call me because she didn't have to.*

I was beginning to feel more and more for Brianna. Maybe I would soon pop the question! Now come on, how can I ask a woman I just met to marry me? That's NOT the question I was talking about. Will she be mine? That's the question! I'm ready to give this a shot. Exclusivity is what I want. Only me in her life and only her in mine. I honestly feel that I am ready. Chapter 3 is about to take place and I want Brianna to be a part of that. I'm ready to give her all of my love—all of my trust. I'm ready to be IN love, and not just SAY "I love you" with no meaning, no real passion.

Who knows, maybe one day I WILL ask her to be Mrs. McCallister, but that time is not now. I'm still learning how to love.

A few days have gone by and Brianna and I have spent countless hours on the phone. We shared feelings, we shared emotions. We talked about everything from having children to what it would be like to grow old together. We talked about our plans for life before we came into each others' life. It was plain to see that we really wanted to be with each other. I didn't know how to ask her about us becoming one. Actually, the last time I literally ASKED a female to be mine, was in high school when I asked Miriam. Anyone else just ASSUMED it was them and I, but I would never commit because I didn't want to be held accountable for anything I did outside of whatever type of relationship they thought we had. A woman could never tell me I cheated on her, even though some would, but deep down inside they had to know that cheating on them wasn't the case because there was never a commitment, not on my part anyway.

I was spending most of my work week on the phone with Brianna. We would talk all day. I was still able to get my work done, but most decisions I had to make were pushed off to the Operations Manager. I had other things on my mind. I bounced around the office like a kid at a circus. A few of my co-workers noticed and asked me what had gotten into me. "Nothing, what are you talking about?" would be my standard answer. I no longer went to lunch with other females and I was not taking anyone else's phone calls. No emails were being returned.

Brianna didn't work days, so it was easy to spend the day with her either on the phone, or she would meet me at the office and we would go out to lunch together. We honestly acted like we were a married couple that had been together for years. One day while we were out, I popped the question.

I felt kinda funny asking her this because like I said, I never had to before. "Bri, I want to ask you something." "What is it Jay? Is everything Ok?" she asked. "Everything is wonderful!" I said. "Ever since you entered my life, things have really been happening with me that I can honestly say has never happened before. It's obvious that you and I like each other. I really like you a lot and I believe you feel the same way about me." She began to touch my face with her right hand. I gently began kissing her fingers as I spoke. "I want you Brianna. I want us. I want us to become one with each other. I am not seeing anyone else, I am not speaking to anyone else, I am not thinking about anyone else. I can't even imagine my life being with anyone else but you. I have never been so sure about anything in my life. I want you to know that I prayed about this before I decided to bring this to you and God told me it was Ok. He told me that my heart was safe with you, and I want nothing more right now than to take this relationship to the next level. That is of course, if you want the same thing in return." Brianna was so emotional. It's like I can feel her heart when she looks at me a certain way.

She looked at me and she smiled. It took her a few minutes before she was able to say anything, and I began to worry that she would say that she is not ready. How would I handle it if that's what she said? Subconsciously I had already begun my rejection reaction. "Jay, I think you are a wonderful man! The first night I met you, when I got home that night, I thanked God for bringing you into my life. I have been yours Jay since the first night you held me close to you on the dance floor. I've just been waiting for you to ask me baby!" She was touching my lips as she spoke. I swear I had never been an emotional type of person when it came to relationships because as I stated, my heart would stay under lock and key, but as she was speaking, I felt her. While she was talking to me and touching my lips at the same time, I was so absorbed by her that my eyes began to water. Boy, if the fellas knew this! At that time, all that mattered was Brianna and I. I didn't even care if I had friends or not. Bri was going to be my best friend anyway! Oh yeah, I'm about to go ALL the way in! "Yes Jay!" "I will be yours, all yours and only yours! I just need one thing from you...." "What's that baby?" I asked. "I will be yours now and always if you promise to trust and believe in me forsaking all others till death do us part." "I do!" I said. "Then by the powers invested in me, by you, I now pronounce us boyfriend and girlfriend!" "You may kiss me." We must've kissed for what felt like five minutes without even coming up for air!

"Wow!" I have a boo!

Chapter 7

Temptations

Days and weeks had passed and Brianna and I grew closer and closer together. I even introduced her to mom. She immediately loved Bri and took to her right away. Everything was going well. We had many more picnics, long drives and relaxing walks in her neighborhood. Walking, holding hands…making future plans together. Why is it when things seem to be at their best, the devil becomes busy? He decided to try me. Her name was Terry. Terry was a blast from the past. She was someone I did have a physical relationship with. Terry and I had history. We were together, she wanted more, I didn't, and she got married and had more children. She already had one (no, not by me). What makes it so bad, is that her husband had the same last name as I did so yes, her name was Terry McCallister but he and I were of no relation whatsoever.

It was a Saturday afternoon and Brianna and I were out at the mall, strolling, holding hands, and standing in line for an Ice cream flavored yogurt or whatever it was and I felt a poke in the ribs. It was Terry, looking as good as ever. "Hey stranger," I turned around and saw that sly grin on her face. Now I am going to try and be as honest as possible here, but the minute I realized who it was, certain feelings began to come over me. Some things you never forget and Terry was one of those unforgettable individuals. She left a lasting impression. I was really upset when I found out she had gotten married. She was tired of waiting around for me, she told me one day a while back. "T...what's up girl?" trying not to act too happy to see her! "T. let me introduce you to my sweetheart, Brianna this is an old friend of mine Terry, Terry this is my lady Brianna."

You could tell by the look on Brianna's face that she didn't trust Terry. I was always told that women can 'sense' when another woman is on the prowl. "Nice to meet you," Terry said trying her best to be polite as possible. Believe me, I know Terry. She is one of those sisters that simply do not care about anything or anyone as long as she gets hers. "Nice to meet you too," said Brianna. "Bri, Terry and I go way back. Her brother and I used to hang out together when I was in high school. Her brother drowned in a swimming pool accident and Terry and I have been really close ever since." Brianna started to ease back a little bit as if she felt it was Ok to let her guard down. "So, what have you been doing with yourself T.?" I asked. "Well, I'm sure you remember but I was married and...." "How's that working out?" I cut her off in mid sentence, and not really sure why I asked, because I cared or because I wanted to see if she was available. "It didn't work out. Child I divorced that fool after the first year. He had the nerve to have this tramp up in my bed while I was at work. My neighbor called me one morning while I was hard at work and told me that there were two cars in my driveway and one of them weren't mine. It only took seven minutes before there were three! Everything went out the window child; suits, hats, silk shirts, everything. I've been happily single ever since." Brianna gets back into the conversation. "So do you live out here?" she asked Terry. "Actually I don't, I moved upstate New York girl. I didn't want any traces of a black man no where near me if you know what I mean." "So what brings you back?" I asked. "My sister Audra and her boyfriend Paco are getting married tomorrow. After that I am on my way back upstate." Disappointed but happy at the same time, I told her how nice it was to see her again and I wished her well. As she walked away she turned around and gave me this look. Fellas know the look. It's that look when you catch her eyes and all you see is "this ain't over." I swear the first thing Brianna asked me after she left was "did you ever sleep with her?" I gave her that look.... "What?" "Where did that come from?" I said sounding like a third grader caught cheating on a test. "She and I never really had a relationship...no, that was never it at all. We're just friends." "I didn't ask you sweetie if you and her had a relationship, I asked if you ever screwed her?" Brianna asked, with the sweetest little look you can ever imagine. "We did a few things." I said in my ghetto, yeah I'm the man tone. "Oh, a few things huh? I see." Brianna had nothing to worry about. She could definitely hold her own against ANY woman, but it's just something different when you have a partner who would do just about anything, anyway...a real freak! Meet Terry!!

This would be the first time I would have to come to terms with whether or not I was in love as much as I thought I was with Brianna. I expected the time to come one day, but not now. I wasn't certain how I would handle it. Deal with life on life's terms, is what I had to keep telling myself. If I am happy, and really care for this woman, I don't need anything extra. I am not one to be naïve to the fact that I expected this change to come overnight, or even in a matter of weeks or months. This would take total reprogramming, but at least I had begun the process. Now this!

The fellas and I had planned to go out that Saturday night. Brianna had to work anyway, so the plan was on. We had planned to go to the arcade and indulge in some 9-ball, but the plan didn't quite go that way. I've had the same phone number for quite a while now, and anyone who knew me, knew how to get in touch with me. As I got out of the shower, still drippin' wet, the phone rang.

"Hello"... "Hey Jay, it's me Terry!" I wrapped a towel around me and sat down on the edge of the bed. "What's up T.?" "Since it's going to be my last night in town, I was hoping we could hook up, maybe go to a Jazz club or

something. I brought this new dress today from the mall, and I am dying to show it off." "H, h...hold on a sec" *I said in a panic.* "Man! NOW what am I gonna do?" *This was the first sign of maturation. In the past, I wouldn't have even given it a second thought.* "Cool," *I said reluctantly but still rather eager.* "Why don't you meet me at my house in an hour," *I told her.* "Don't worry, I remember the way. It should only take me 45 min." "Cool" *Man, did I feel guilty. Brianna is out at work making a living, and I'm getting ready to go out with someone I had a sexual history with. Ok, a STRONG sexual history with! Now I gotta call the fellas. I'll call D, since it's always easier to get out of things through him, and let him do the explaining for me.*

(hello) "What's up D?" "I ain't ready yet man, you gotta give me about an hour. It's 2nd quarter and I'm down by a field goal. I ain't even BEGIN to get dressed yet." "Man, put the controller down and come back into the real world! You and that damn playstation. I'm calling to tell you that I'm not coming tonight my brother. I'm beat man, so I'm going to rent a video and call it a night." *I can't tell Darryl or any of the fellas about Terry. As much as I've been pumping up how much of a changed man I am, they would never let me hear the end of it if I told them that I was going out with her. They knew Terry. They would know that if Terry and I hooked up it would deter my development.* "Personally, I think you just don't wanna lose any money tonight, but whatever man, I'll let T. and Curt know. Let me go, my team is noticing that I am distracted." "Wow!" "You're starting to scare me my brother. I'll get with you tomorrow." "Yeah, yeah, tomorrow."

It's 10 minutes to 9 and all I can think about is Brianna...and Terry. I guess you're not understanding me. This thing is NOT easy! I'm smelling good, looking my best and KNOW that I'm wrong. (phone rings) "Hey baby!" *It's Brianna!* "Are you on your way out?" *she asked. I felt as if she KNEW what I was getting ready to do.* "Yeah, yeah I'm almost ready. D. and Curt should be here in a minute and T-mac will meet us there." *I said very unconvincingly.* "Ok baby, have a good time and think about me Ok?" "How could I not?" "Jay...I want to tell you something. It's something I've been struggling to get out and just didn't know how to say it, but I need to let you know." *Again, I sit on the edge of the bed not knowing what to expect.* "I really hope you can handle this because I would hate for anything to come between us." "Just tell me baby, we're both adults," *I said not really knowing whether or not I really wanted to hear this.*

I KNEW that something was going to come out that I would not want to hear. I was already happy that I DID decide to hook up with Terry. "I'm in love with you Jay" "Excuse me," *I said not sure of what I thought I just heard.* "I said that I'm in love with you baby!" *Right at that point, I knew I couldn't go out with Terry tonight. I prayed for Brianna, and God blessed me with a beautiful woman that is not only my soul mate but is quickly becoming my best friend, and I was lying to her.* "Say something!" *she said.* "I knew I shouldn't have told you yet," *with the sound of disappointment in her tone.* "Brianna, I seriously had to absorb what you just told me and I cannot begin to tell you how special I feel, and...." "I don't want you to tell me just because I told you," *she stated emphatically.*
"I want you to tell me when you truly feel it." "That's fair enough," *I said.* "Thank you for sharing your feelings with me Brianna. I promise to take real good care of your heart." "Hold on baby," *she says.* "Sweetie I have to go, have fun Ok and remember what I just told you." "I will and be careful. I'll call you when I get in." "Ok" "talk to you then."

No sooner than I hung up the phone the doorbell rang. Man, this is going too fast for me right now. My head is swimming. I heard this saying when I was younger and now I'm beginning to get the true meaning of it; "If it ain't rough, it ain't right!" *I seemed to LIVE by that saying. (bell rings again). I opened the door and Terry kindly nudged me to the side and makes her way in.* "Hey Jay, are you ready?" "Terry, I am not feeling too well. I really do want to go, but I have a serious case of indigestion and I am just not feeling well enough to go out tonight. I think I'm just going to

go get a movie and lie down the rest of the night," I said apologetically. *"Too late, I beat you to it." She opens up her purse and pulls out a DVD. What makes it so bad is it was something I really wanted to see! "I thought we were supposed to go out?"*
I asked her. "What happened to this dress you brought that you wanted to show off?" She pulls off her jacket (it was a little cool at night still) and she had on the tightest, tightest, dress you can ever imagine, and yes it did it look good on her.... REAL GOOD!

She gave me her jacket and I took it in the room to hang it up. While in there, I got down on my knees.... "Jesus, you know I never ask you for things, I'm known for always singing your praises, never wanting to seem selfish or ungrateful, but Lord I need you now. Please intercede here tonight and keep the devil away." Fact is, with that dress, the devil was already in and sitting on my sofa! I walked back into the living room and she stood up and gave me a hug. "Come here boy. You acted like you were scared to show me love earlier. I mean, I know that was your girl and all, but don't act like you forgot what we had and that it wasn't damn good for both of us! That's part of the reason I got a divorce. Hell my husband may have been doing HIS thing, but he wasn't stupid enough to know that I wasn't doing mine too!" "I'm not trying be disrespectful Terry, but it's just not like that right now. I am really into this woman and I'm going to do what I need to do to keep it going just the way it is."

I tried to sound believable. "All of that sounds really good Jay, but this is me!" She took the DVD and placed it inside the DVD player. As she was standing in front of the 52" with the shortest, tightest dress in the mall on her body, all you could see were the curves. It was sheer from the waist down, and in front of the TV it was easy to see that she didn't have on any underwear. She walked over to the windows, which there was one of both sides of the TV, and began to lift them one by one. Boy did the breeze feel good! On her way back to the sofa she unzipped her dress, slid it off, and neatly folded it as she laid it on my recliner. Next she proceeded to lie on my sofa on her stomach. "Terry, what are you doing? Didn't I just tell you that it's not like that anymore? Why are you trying me?" "Because I know what you like and how you like it (licking her fingers slowly)…boy does she!" "Terry, I told you, it's not going down like this! Not now, not tonight, not ever again! If you don't want to be cool with me on a strictly friendship basis, then I guess you may as well leave now," I said feeling I had gotten my point across. "So you're gonna send me back Upstate New York THIS wet?" She sat up on the sofa and spread her legs. (doorbell rings) "Yo Jay!"…the windows were open and it sounded like the voice was right in the next room. "Open the door partner!" "The first voice was Darryl's, the second was Curt's.

"Whos car is in the driveway Jay?"……you guessed it—that was T. "Yo man, we went and got some cards and some crabs. I'ma take your money one way or the other." On my way to the window, Terry said "Tell the fellas I said haaayy," she was all happy, like she WANTS them to know that it's her and that SHE and not Brianna was the one tonight! "Please, just be quiet for a second can you do that for me?" "If you can do something for me!" "Shhhhhhhhh" "Yo man, I'm about to crash for the night fellas. I really ain't up for it tonight!" I tried to get them to believe me. "Who's car is this my man?" T-mac asked me like he KNEW something foul was in the air. "It's someone visiting next door. They asked me if they could park here and I told them it would be Ok. Is that good enough for you Columbo?" All of a sudden I feel Terry's hand on both cheeks of my behind. I had on some loose dress pants, so she was able to get a good grip. I had to fight her off and get rid of these guys at the same time. "What are you doing up there man?" Darryl said. "You got somebody up there don't you?" Now Terry was on the floor, underneath me, trying to unbuckle my pants while I was leaning over in the window. "Listen, I gotta go fellas!" "I'm tired, I'll get with you tomorrow." "Don't let me find out you got someone else up there besides Brianna!" Curt said as they were walking away. Right at that time, I felt Terry's lips kiss my bellybutton. I immediately jumped back and began to buckle my pants. She walked in front of the TV and bent over. "Here Jay, you know you like it this way!" Truth be told, it was looking sooooooo good

and the man in me really struggled with the reasons I had for NOT doing this. If I had sex with this woman tonight, I don't think I would ever be able to look at Brianna the same way again. Out of pure guilt and a sense of betrayal our relationship would never be the same. The feeling I have of how special she was to me would evaporate with that first orgasm because she would then be just like every other woman I had in my past, just there until something else came along. However, this time I did something different…. I thought about how SHE would feel! That's the difference. Before, it would not matter to me how someone else felt. But I cared about Brianna. I could picture the look on her face if she was to find out that I had sex with this woman, the same woman that she had a sneaky suspicion about all along. That would be wrong. "Terry, you really need to put your clothes on. This is not going down tonight." This time she knew I was for real. "I am not trying to disrespect you Jay, and I am not trying to disrespect your lady either, but you and I have that type of friendship. We were ALWAYS there for each other Jay, no matter whom else was in our lives. Hell, I was MARRIED and couldn't stop being with you!" "Why do you want to treat me this way now? I am not asking you to marry me, just satisfy me the way that you were always so good at doing!" "I understand that Terry, and I really appreciate what we had, but things have changed." "I still care about you and you will always be my girl, but I have a woman in my life now that I was blessed enough to have God deliver to me and I am not willing to chance losing that over sex." "It's just that simple." Terry put on her dress and I think she was kind of embarrassed. That is the first time I ever saw her face flush.

"Listen Terry, what we had was great and I still hope we can continue to be friends, but it's all about Brianna now and she has to be my priority, she has to come even before my own wants and needs." "I can respect that Jay. You'll always be my boy. She is a very lucky woman. Not only will she be getting the best sex this part of the East coast, but she will have something no other woman before her has ever had, not since I've known you anyway…your heart!"

Terry kissed me on the cheek and I walked her to the door. She gave me a hug and we shook hands. "This will always be between you and I Jay. Take care baby." "You too T. Stay safe!"

Man, I felt like a million dollars! I felt like going outside and running around the block that's how happy I was. I DID IT!! I was able to turn down sex from Terry!! Now I KNOW things have changed! I really need to speak to Brianna. Let me call her. ("hello you know who you've reached, leave a message at the tone") "Brianna, call me baby when you get a minute." Come on now, don't be crazy. Why would I tell her I turned down sex with Terry? Of course I wasn't calling to tell her that. I wanted her to know something...something I've been dying to say to someone for so long, and really mean it. Yes, I wanted to tell Brianna that I was in love with her too!

Chapter 8

It was time

After passing the ultimate test on love and monogamy, something came to mind that actually hadn't even been a thought…sex! Brianna and I had a 'different' type of relationship. We were both Christians, and sex before marriage is an unjust action, something that is not supposed to happen. We believed that with all we had been through in the past, we didn't want to do anything to jeopardize the blessings we prayed for God to bestow upon our relationship. We both were looking for future…for substance, for a relationship that goes against the grain from what this world today has brainwashed us into believing is acceptable. See, if Brianna was just another woman that I was getting to know, and if sex was something that happened to come up while we were 'dating,' then that was Ok. I wasn't making that person my future. I didn't have plans of proposal and marriage, and I certainly wasn't standing before God give him my word that I would love that woman forever. It was just something to do. One of those sins that I would be forgiven for. Don't get me wrong, I do know that no one sin is greater than the other, but by comparison, that type of 'casual sex' if I had to compare it to a crime, would be a misdemeanor. I would be slapped with a fine and told to be on my way. I had plans for Brianna. This was not a 'casual' thing, this was real! Do I really want to risk our blessings for a night or many nights of unmarried, lustful although filled with love, sexual indiscretions with the one I love?

After four months of Brianna and I being together, we had begun the transition of staying over at each others houses. On any given night (when Brianna didn't have to work of course), either she would be at my place or I would be at hers. I had keys to her house and she had keys to mine. We also had keys to each others' car. This was definitely a first, but we were always thinking ahead, just in case one or the other would lose or misplace their keys, we had each other's back. Yes, this was totally different but it was all good and I was loving it! I will admit that lying there at night, holding such a beautiful woman in my arms, her head lying on my bare chest, was really hard. Some nights were easier than others. Those nights when I was really tired, I just wanted to sleep anyway, but the nights when I had energy and she would be asleep by nine or ten at night, I would put in DVD after DVD and watch movie after movie until I fell asleep.

We would also have our romantic evenings as well…dinner, wine, soft music, slow dancing, and lots and lots of physical affection, just never all the way. Brianna made it kind of easy on me. She would always sleep in long pajamas or as I would call them, her grandmamma night gowns.

Brianna must have caught a vibe between Terry and I the day before at the mall, and when I confessed that she was someone that I HAD slept with, Brianna began to change. I noticed it the night after the Terry episode.

We had gone to church that morning, and had a wonderful afternoon out with my children Brandon and Kayla who both absolutely loved Brianna and took to her almost immediately. After spending the day with the kids, we went back to Bri's house later on that night. The minute we walked in I sensed something different. First of all, she opened the door. That never happened. She would always allow me to open the door and to go in first. Not this particular night. "Hold on baby, let me do that" she said. I stepped back and as she entered and poked her head in the door, I noticed lights flickering, as if there was a fire in the living room. "Baby what is that?" I asked already thinking about what I needed to get out of the house first.... The T.V., DVD Player and my playstation 2! (I had one here and at my house). "It's Ok sweetie, come on in." She opened the door and the whole living room was lit up with candles. "How did you do this and we were out all afternoon and most of this evening?" I asked with a puzzled look on my face. "I told Karen what time to come over and she lit the candles for me. Everything else was already done." She said. "This is beautiful baby, but what's the special occasion?" hoping I didn't forget something. Was it our four month anniversary? Man, when did I ask her to be mine? What could it be? "The special occasion is that you and I are in love." She had such a look of contentment in her eyes that I felt every word she said. Not only did she have candles lit, but she had a bottle of sparkling cider chillin' on the table, with a bowl of strawberries along with two other bowls, one of whipped cream and the other of chocolate with the little tea light underneath it. There were rose petals all over the living room sofa and a trail leading to the bedroom.

"There is another reason for me extending extra effort tonight Jay. I want you to sit back and relax." She began to unbutton the top of my shirt. After unbuttoning the top three or four buttons, she unlaced my sneakers and slid off my socks. She then placed slippers on my feet. "Are you comfortable sweetie?" she asks. "Very baby, is everything Ok?" I didn't ask her that because this was unusual for Brianna. No, she would regularly make a brother feel like he was King in his castle AND her castle. She would always be 'willing' to be the Queen and accept that role proudly, whether at my house OR hers. She didn't have to be in control. She didn't have to be in charge. She didn't mind stepping back and taking on the role of the woman, even though she had been on her own for quite some time only having her to depend on and only used to doing things for herself. All I had to do was show her that I knew how to handle mine, and she was all for

giving up the control she was so used to having which went against what she was taught.

"Every night we're together is a special occasion baby but yes, tonight is a little different," she continued. *Boy I hope I didn't forget anything.* "Jay, ever since you came into my life, my whole world has changed. When I first met you, that first night at the club, I had no idea how much a part of my life you would become. I really had good feelings then, but I really didn't know until our first 'real' date that this was something special, something different." "Do you remember where you took me on our first date Jay?" "Of course I do, we went to Ray-Ray's Rib Shack for breakfast!" "What was so special about that Bri?" "What am I going to do with you Jason?!" "No, it wasn't Ray-Ray's, it was to church BEFORE Ray-Ray's Mr. Romantic!" "I was just kiddin' baby, I remembered." "Yeah right! Anyway silly, you are a really good man Jay and I am really blessed to have a man like you in my life. Not only do I love you, but I trust you. I trust that in everything I do you've got me, that you've got my back. I feel safe with you and the little things you do to show me that you are in love with me and that I am always on your mind, mean more to me than any thing anyone else has ever done for me, brought for me, taken me, or anything else. For the first time in my life I know what true love feels like. I can be me. I can be Brianna without being questioned, judged or taken for granted. I know you and I have abstained from physical intimacy, but I want you Jay. I want you tonight. I am ready to take that next step with you. I don't want to wait any longer to experience you in the flesh. My body and my mind cannot take it any longer, but there's one more thing…" She took my hand and led me into the bedroom. In the middle of a pile of rose petals in the middle of the bed was a box with a ribbon on it. It wasn't a big box, but it wasn't a small box either. I sat on the bed and I took the box in my hand. Brianna was standing over me. "Go ahead, open it. It is a present from me to you," She said smiling. I untied the ribbon and opened the box. It was a Rolex watch. "Baby!" "you didn't have to buy me a watch like this!" "It's beautiful, but you really didn't have to! I know how much you love me and no *material object is going to make me think you love me anymore than I already do. I don't want to sound unappreciative, but I really can't take this from you."* Again, the maturation process was in the works. Anytime in the past if a woman would have brought me a Timex, I would have felt like 'the man,' but this woman purchased me a Rolex and I didn't even want to take it! *"I am not trying to 'buy' your love Jay. I am just trying to show you how much you mean to me." "Please, take it out the box and put it on. I want to see how it looks on you."* As I took it out the box, something else fell out and hit the floor. *"What was that?"* I asked. Brianna bent down to pick whatever it was up off the floor. As I was admiring the watch on my arm, she took me by the hand. *"Jayson McCallister, I never want to be without you in my life."* She said with a tear in her eye. *"I want to wake up next to you, in your arms every morning. I want to love you forever and ever till death do us part. I want to grow old with you.... Jason, will you marry me?"* She slid a platinum band on my ring finger and gently kissed it afterwards. I had forgotten all about the Rolex. I was speechless to say the least! The last time I felt like this I was 4 yrs old and I was sitting on Santa's lap and he handed me a present. When I opened that present it was something I had asked my mom for all year and she kept putting me off. It was my first pair of Pro-Keds! I kinda felt the same way, but on a much more mature level. I mean, I wasn't going to run around the house in the dark, yelling and screaming as I did when I got those sneakers, but I was just as overwhelmed…and I was overwhelmed with emotion. A tear ran down my left cheek as I thought about the beauty of this woman. *"Are you for real Brianna?" "Are you really proposing to ME?" "With us Jay, it is not about what is 'typically' done. Everything with us is based on how we feel about situations. We don't allow society to dictate how we live our lives. We follow only one law and what is written in the Holy Bible is that law. That is what I love so much about our relationship. We do what we feel we need to do for each other, not what society says we should do."* She continued… *"Baby, I have never been more serious in my life, about anything!" "If you need some time to consider, then I will understand that and I will give you all the time you need, so long as you know my proposal will always stand." She seemed a little disappointed that I hadn't answered her yet, but my mind was still rockin' from the thought of this woman being my wife! "Brianna, I would be the dumbest man in the world to wait another ten seconds to answer you." "Of course I will marry you baby...my answer is YES."*

I lifted her up off of the floor as she sat on my lap and threw her arms around my neck. Passionately we kissed. I laid back on the bed as she crawled on top of me and began to unbutton the remaining buttons that were still fastened on my shirt. Gently she began to kiss my neck.

We both knew full well the consequences of sex before marriage, but the temptation was just too great. The mood, the moment...it was all so perfect. Besides, we were 'engaged' to be married right? Any way to justify the feelings that we both shared would be enough for us that night. Brianna and I made love for the first time and it was more beautiful than even she was. It's a difference when you make love someone you are actually "in-love" with. There's more heart, more feeling, more passion. I felt every single movement, every motion was a motion that was meant and afterwards we'd lay in each others arms as if the world belonged to us.

Chapter 9

▼

The ATL...

A month after the engagement, Brianna and I decided we wanted to take a trip. I had a partner from Jersey that had moved to Atlanta about three years before Bri came along. His name was Kenny. Kenny and his wife Monica and their children had moved to the land of opportunity to begin a better life. They had a house built just for them and he loved it. Kenny and I used to work together for a while before one day he told me that he was going to move to the Atl. At first I didn't believe him, but when he gave his notice to our boss, I knew he was serious. I had been to Atlanta before on business, but never to just hang out. I also had a few relatives there, one that I hadn't seen in quite a while (he was my brothers age) and one I had never seen. She was my mom's cousin.

The dog days of summer up North were now turning into the cool, brisk days of fall, and I wanted just a little bit more of the warmth that Atlanta still had at this time of year. Kenny did tell me that anytime I wanted to come down to just let him know but see, Kenny knew me from back then...you know, the one who could never give his heart to a woman. He had no idea what was going on when I called him. "Kenny my man, what's going on fella?" "I know this ain't Jay," he said with a sound of disbelief. "What's up special K?" "I wanted to see what you had planned for the com-

ing weekend. I really need to get out of Jersey for a few days and was considering flying down to the 'dirty-dirty' south to see what's going on in YOUR part of the country!" "Actually, this weekend would be really good. Monica and I are celebrating our 7 year wedding anniversary and I'm sure she would love to see you too." "Cool, count us in." "Us?" Kenny said sounding confused. "Oh yeah, I haven't spoken to you in a while have I? Ya boy is doing big things," I said with the sound of contentment in my voice. "Oh boy, who is it this time?" "Her name is Brianna, we're actually engaged to be married!" "What!?" "Stop playin!" Kenny knew of my past escapades and would never ever believe that I was finally settling down, unless he saw it for himself. He probably wouldn't believe it until he was standing there at the wedding, tux and all as one of the groomsmen and probably not even then. "Yeah man, Brianna is a wonderful woman and I would definitely say I lucked up on this one. She actually proposed to ME!" "What?...yeah you gotta come down now my man. Wait until I tell Monica THIS!"

Friday morning came and Brianna and I were preparing our things for the weekend. Our flight was scheduled to leave at 4:35 pm from Newark Airport to Hartsfield in Atlanta. Kenny was gonna meet us there. "Are you sure you have everything sweetie," Brianna asked. "I think so, and what I don't have I can get when we get there. You know the weather is still hot there, so please don't pack any of those hot long sleeve sweaters you wear," I told her "and bring a bathing suit, I wanna show those 'bout it-'bout it brothers down there what it's REALLY about up North!" Atlanta is known as the land of milk and honey, well known for big booty sisters and Kenny would always make it a point to tell me what I was missing being up North. I just wanted to show him that what I had could stand up to anything they had in the "A."

The plan was for Brianna and I to stop by my mom's house as she was making breakfast for us, run to the mall and pick up a few things then we would be on our way to the airport.

Breakfast at my mom's was great. Eggs & cheese, grits, toast, sausage and orange juice. Mom knew how hook a son up! Her and Brianna washed dishes as I called Darryl and asked him to keep an eye on my apartment for me. After we kissed mom goodbye we were on our way to the mall. On our way there, Brianna asked me if I could make a quick stop. She needed to check on a few things regarding her job. Brianna never spoke much about her job and I never pushed her on it. I knew she was in the entertainment industry and I had an idea that it was in some sort of managing aspect, but I am not one to smother someone about what they do, I never was. Obviously, it was something that was really paying off for her with the way she was living. Even in the past, I would not call women at work. I would never want to disturb someone at their place of business, and I generally would not want to be disturbed at mine, except now of course.

We pulled up at this nice-fancy club looking type of place that had valet parking and the whole nine. "I will only be a few minutes baby." She kissed me on the cheek and dashed off. This must be some kind of place, this was midday and the parking lot was packed! Mainly, there seemed to be guys coming and going but there were quite a few couples walking in and out also. "What kind of place has this type of business in the middle of the day?" I wondered. As I looked around for a Marquee or something thinking maybe I can see who was performing, all I saw was a sign with the name of the club on it… **" The Crystal Palace "** *Personally, I've never heard of it, but it really seems to be a big time place. Five minutes later, Brianna came out. She spent a few minutes laughing with the valet guys and got back in the car. "Is everything Ok," I asked her. "Yes sweetie, everything's fine. I just had to check on a few things before we left." "What type of club is this?" I asked. "Just a regular club," she said matter of factly. "I mean, no one is in there getting butt naked on the tables or anything like that is it?" I asked. "You are so silly Jay," she laughed. We both laughed.*

We arrived in Atlanta as scheduled. Kenny was there to greet us with this big grin on his face. "Jaaaaaaayyyyy my man, what's up?" Kenny said in that high pitched voice of his. "What's up special K? Brianna this is Kenny, Kenny this is my fiancée Brianna." "Nice to meet you Kenny," Brianna said in that soft silky voice of hers. "Nice to meet you too Ms. Brianna. I was gonna ask you how'd you finally hook this guy, but trust me, I don't even need to ask!" Kenny gave me that look like I landed Halle Berry! "Can you guys give me a second, I drank so much water on the plane that it feels like I am carrying a baby in my stomach. I'll be right back. Which way is the ladies room." Kenny pointed her in the right direction. "Daaammmmnnnn!" "How did you pull THAT off?" Kenny asked. "I see why you said yes!" "I would have slapped you if you would have said no to THAT!" "Brianna is more than just gorgeous, she is really a classy woman that really knows how to treat a man." "You know me Kenny, I have had a really hard time totally believing in a woman, but from the first night Brianna and I met, it was on. She's smart, sexy, loving, caring, trustworthy, funny, God fearing AND is her own boss. What more can a man ask for?" Kenny nodded his head in agreement. He and Monica had been thru hell and back but as of our last conversation, they were finally getting it all together. "So grillmaster, what are you planning to put on the grill tomorrow?" I asked. "You know me, I can shut down a meat market. I got it all, you name it, chicken, ribs, steak, burger, dogs, chops...."

Brianna made her way back from the ladies room and we were on our way.
"It's been so long since I've been to Atlanta," said Brianna. "The last time I was here was during freaknik. Me and a few crazy girlfriends of mine were young and adventurous and was stuck in traffic on—what's the main highway out here?" "85?" asked Kenny. "Yeah, that's it, 85. We were in traffic for maybe 4-5 hours. Cars were just parked on the highway and boy was it wild! Mardi gra had NOTHING on freaknik!" She seemed as though she had drifted back to those days in her mind. "I guess you had your booty shakin' out the window too huh?" I asked. "Oh, cut it out...what's wrong baby, you're jealous?" "Whatever Bri...I'm your freaknik now, that's all that matters." "That's right baby." She leaned up

and put her arms around my neck. I was riding in the front seat and she was behind me. "We are staying at the 'W' in perimeter Kenny. Can you take us by to pick up a rent-a-car first and show us the way to the hotel? Tonight we are just gonna chill, spend some time at the Hotel and get up with you and Monica tomorrow cool?" "Cool" The 'W' is my SPOT! Every time I went to the Atl. on business, I would stay at the 'W'. I love their far eastern theme. It was romantic in a unique kinda way. I couldn't wait to get Brianna there! She had never been there. By the time we picked up our car and got to the hotel, it was almost 9 o'clock. I had reserved a three-room suite on the 7th floor with a balcony outside the bedroom that had a view of the Atlanta skyline. The minute we got off the elevator on our floor, which was dimly lit with purple wall lights, Brianna was in awe. "Wow, this is beautiful!" she said. "Oh, you haven't seen anything yet." I said feeling like a kid on my way to se a Bruce lee movie (that was my favorite thing to do as a kid). I slid the key in the door and when I opened it, the first view we had entering the living room was the skyline. The blinds were open and it was beautiful! Brianna walked in and immediately kicked off her shoes and jumped on the plush leather sofa that sat in front of the big bay windows in the living room. She looked down and saw the pool, the hot tub to her right, and the hotels restaurant to the left. She got up and began to walk around in the room, marveling at every piece of exotic décor the room had to offer. The square Asian sink in the bathroom with the funky toilet bowl—made you WANNA take a…well, you know what I mean. The kitchen with the Asian style sink and the beautifully crafted plates and glasses. Then she walked into the bedroom and noticed the bottle of wine that was chillin' in a bucket of ice, sitting on the unusually shaped nightstand next to the bed. Room service had sent it up as requested at 8pm as I figured we would not arrive there until around 9. She looked around the amazingly stylish and lavish bedroom opening draws, closets, and anything else that would open. Finally, she noticed the ceiling—to—floor length vertical blinds that covered the balcony. She walked over, pulled them open and slid back the sliding glass door. As she stepped onto the balcony, I walked out behind her and put my arms around her waist. She laid her *head back into my chest and closed her eyes. A breeze was blowing, the sky was clear. Downtown Atlanta never looked so beautiful! We shared a kiss. We shared many kisses on the balcony.*

After a while, I led her back inside. "Why don't we change into our pool gear, grab something really quick to eat downstairs, and go relax in the hot tub," I asked. "Anything you want baby," she said. I had never seen Brianna look so relaxed. I mean, she always had it going on, but tonight there was a certain type of relaxed feeling in her face, in her manner, and in her tone, like I had slipped her a mickey or something, but I knew what it was…it was the 'W', it had that type of effect on newcomers. Trust me, I was the same way my first night there, but I was alone and ended up going to sleep.

After a bite to eat we slipped into the outdoor Jacuzzi. Me first then Brianna as she sat on the step in front of me between my legs. The water was practically up to her neck as she rested her head in my chest. Boy, this felt sooooo goooood! Being in love, totally in love, really in love and my woman in my arms in the Jacuzzi at the 'W' in Atlanta. What more can a man ask for? After a while in the Jacuzzi, I wanted to go back to the room. In the elevator going up, we began to get passionate once again. When the elevator doors opened, I picked her up and carried her to the room, kissing her all the way. Once inside the room, I turned on some soft music as Brianna got in the shower. After taking care of some business I had in the room, I joined her. Again we were passionate…very passionate. After the shower we dried each other off and I got the square shaped glasses for our wine. We sat on the sofa in our bathrobes as I poured both of our glasses half-way. "A toast to our love," I said. We touched glasses. "Before we drink, I have something to show you," I said. I stood her up and walked her into the bedroom. In the bedroom in the middle of the bed was a box. I asked her to pick it up as I led her back to the balcony. On the balcony, in our bathrobes, I told her to open it. She opened the box and placed her hand over her mouth. It was the most beautiful, platinum princess cut dia-

mond ring you can imagine. It was 2 ½ carats in the center with a total of 2 carats on the sides. I took it out of the box, and got down on one knee.

"Baby, you have come into my life and changed my whole outlook on what I believed love was all about. Before you, I had no idea of what love should feel like. I was afraid, like a child in a strange place. You have put my fears to rest with the love you've given me freely and shown me daily. I would have never imagined that God would bless me in such a way. The material things that were placed in my life were what I considered a blessing, until you came along. You are a blessing…you are MY blessing, and I would be honored to be your husband and to have you as my wife. I know we went thru this already and I have already said yes I will be your husband, but God spoke to me and spoke into me that my knee too shall bow and not only ask you to be my wife, but to praise his name for bringing you into my life. Thank you Jesus! Brianna, will you marry me?" Tears streamed down her face as she said yes. I stood and we embraced. We walked back into the bedroom and we embraced again…this time for the rest of the night.

CHAPTER 10

THE COOKOUT

(Phone rings)—"Hello"—"What's up Jay, it's Kenny." "What time are you and Brianna coming through because I have a few things to do and I wanted to know what time I should come and meet you so that you can follow me back to the house?" "What time is it now," I asked, still tired from a long night of Brianna. "It's 11am my brother, were you still asleep?" "Not really, but we did just wake up." "Be here around 12:30 I guess if that's Ok." "Yeah, that's a good time for me, so I'll see you then. Peace." Brianna was still asleep. I gently kissed her on the lips. "Wake up honey! Let's go downstairs and grab some breakfast before Kenny gets here." "What time is it," she asked with one eye half open. "It's 11 baby, come on." "Ok, Ok" We both got out of bed and took turns in the shower. After a quick pot of coffee, we were on our way downstairs for breakfast. Kenny showed up about 12:45 and we followed him to his house which was about 30 minutes away from the Hotel. As we pulled into his driveway, his three kids were in the front yard playing. "Uncle J, Uncle J!" They came running over and attacked the car like window washers on the side of the George Washington Bridge. "Hold on girls, let me get out!" The youngest was Kennedy, she was my girl. Kennedy was 11 going on 28. Then there was Kira who was 13 and finally Sara who was 14. "Who is that?" asked Kennedy with her hands on her hips in her grown 28 yr old tone. "This is Brianna, Kennedy…this is my future wife!" "Brianna this is Kennedy!"

"I see your little butt hasn't changed have you?" "No, and I aint gone to!" "Watch it Kennedy!" Monica yelled out from the window above the garage. "Hey guurll," I yelled up to Monica. "Hey Jay-Hi Brianna!" "Come on up girl!" Brianna gave me a kiss and walked up the stairs followed closely by Kennedy, who was watching her every step. I'm sure she had a thousand questions for Brianna. Kennedy was my personal screener. When they still lived In Jersey, if I took a woman to meet Kenny and Monica I would make sure Kennedy was around. If they could survive Kennedy then they had a chance with me. Usually, she would break 'em down and that would let me know whether or not they had a backbone. Kenny and I stayed outside while Brianna went in to meet Monica. "So how do you like it out here?" I asked. "Man, I love it! This is what life is supposed to be. Do you know how much I paid to have this house built?" he asked. "$145,000 and we have 4 bedrooms, 2 ½ bathrooms, a two-car garage AND a full basement!" "My property tax is less than $1000 a year! Tell me where up North would I have gotten something like this for a price like that?" "Downtown Elizabeth!" I told him, "right across the street from the projects!" we laughed.

Kenny lived in a subdivision of neatly manicured lawns and trimmed hedges. Everyone knew everyone else. It was real cool, a real family type atmosphere. Much different than where he lived in Jersey where sirens and gunshots were a regular. Yeah, Kenny came up. "This is really nice man. I'm proud of you!" "Thanks Jay, it really feels good my brother. Come on, let me show you the inside."

After seeing all there was to see on the inside, we made our way to the backyard where this dude had three grills set up. Grill number one was a basic, charcoal grill. Grill number two was a gas grill. Grill number three was the biggie. 'The Big Burger Buster 3500'(that was just a name I made up).

This was one of those big drums cut in half with a wire grill on top. It smoked like a chimney and you could see and smell the smoke from miles away. Brianna and Monica were in the house talking, talking about me I believe. The minute we walked in they got quiet. "Why'd you girls get quiet?" I asked. They both had smiles on their faces. "Ain't nobody talkin' about you boy," said Monica in her countriest of voices. Yeah, she was definitely from the south now. "Come here and give me a hug." Monica was my girl. She was a bit chatty at times, but she was good people. "Help me take this meat outside Jay," she asked. I know what that meant, she wanted to get me alone. "Here, grab this tray." Once outside, she started. "Brianna seems like a really nice girl Jay. Kenny told me you had gotten engaged. How long have you known her?" "It's been about six months now," I said sounding as if I was answering my mom instead of my friend. "Do you love her? Wait, let me rephrase that…are you IN love with her?" "Definitely Monica, Brianna is special. I know you and Kenny think you guys know me, but this is different. She is a wonderful woman, a woman that was brought into my life for a reason, and I would cut off my right hand before I do anything to hurt or disappoint her," I said in my most believable voice. "Sounds good," she said. "But I hope you are truly for real this time. God keeps giving you chance after chance Jay with really good women, but you always manage to mess it up. What's different this time?" "I'm 30 years old Monica.

If I don't get it together now, I'll never get it together. I'm tired of running—tired of not trusting—of being afraid to love. Eventually, I have to trust someone and Brianna is my someone. She's here for life!" She reached out and gave me a hug. "You're a good man Jay, and Kenny and I just wanna see you happy." "I appreciate that sweetie. You know you guys will have to come to Jersey for the wedding, whenever we get around to setting the date that is." "Just let Kenny know and we'll be there," she said. "You have to come, you know I'm counting on you to do the singing, and Kenny is going to be one of the groomsmen." Monica could blow! That girl was blessed with a voice! I was at her and Kenny's wedding and she sang to him before they took their vows. There wasn't a dry eye in the house by the time she was done. Me, I cried like a baby!

Kenny and Brianna came out of the house followed closely by Kennedy of course. "Baby, Brianna said she knows how to play spades and bid whist," Kenny said to Monica. "You know what THAT mean...later on IT'S on!" "By the way Kenny and Monica, Happy Anniversary," said Brianna. "When Jay and I have OUR seven year anniversary, maybe you'll let us have the party here," Brianna said. "No doubt," Kenny blurted out. "Anything to give him a reason to fire up those grills. He'll probably have six by then," said Monica. We all laughed. "Ya'll crazy," said Kennedy "I'm going in the front." Kennedy would hang with grown-ups because her conversation was too sophisticated for kids.

"So, who's coming to the cookout?" I asked. "Everybody," said Kenny. "It should be about 40-50 people here later on." "Wow!" "Are you going to uncover the pool?" I asked. "Ya know it," Kenny said all proud like. "I have to run back to the grocery store. Wanna come Brianna?" Monica asked. "Only if Kennedy can come with us," Brianna laughed. "You know she can't stay here with the children anyway." We all laughed. Brianna gave me a kiss and they were on their way.

As promised, the Anniversary barbecue was laced with people. Some of which I knew, most of which I hadn't. The only ones I did know were Kenny and Monica's relatives from up North. There were two spades tables, a bid whist table and a table of old maid for the kids. Brianna and I were sitting by the pool with our feet in the water. Kids were jumping up and splashing repeatedly. Kenny and Monica were playing spades. "Yo Jay, why don't you put more meat on the grill!" Kenny shouted to me, as if the 50 lbs already cooked weren't enough. "Ok man, I got it." "I'll be right back baby" I went into the kitchen, grabbed a tray and loaded more meat onto it. As I was bringing it out, I glanced over at the pool and noticed this brother who had been eyeing Brianna all night, now sitting next to her.

My first impulse was to run over there with the tray and smack him upside the head with it, meat and all, but I decided I would watch for a minute and see how this would unfold.

I really couldn't hear the conversation but I could tell Brianna was becoming a bit agitated simply by her movements alone. The more she slid to the left, the more he slid to the left. She turned around and saw me watching. By now I was just standing there with my hand on my chin, like a leopard waiting to leap. She gave me that look like, "will you come get this fool away from me" but I wanted to see how far he was gonna push her. My baby had a mean streak that only few knew about. Trust me, a woman as fine as Brianna was used to fools coming up to her and if they didn't get the response they hoped for they would act ignorant, so she had a way of dealing with issues like this. A few minutes passed and she started to get angry. He began making hand gestures as if he was telling her that she wasn't all that, which is a brothers favorite line when he gets rejected. I looked over at Kenny and pointed to Brianna and the smooth operator. Kenny waved his hand as if saying, "that dude is harmless man, don't pay it any mind." I turned around to put the meat on the grill and all of a sudden I heard a big splash! Everyone turned around and Billy Dee was in the pool. I neglected to tell you that he was fully dressed AND he couldn't swim. "Help! Yo somebody help me!" He yelled out. Kenny and a few people from the card tables ran over to the side of the pool. Fact is, it was only like a 5 foot pool, so all my man REALLY had to do was stand up and he would've been cool, but he panicked and was gasping for air like a sick seal.

I walked over and Brianna was standing there yelling "don't you EVER put your hands on me!" "He touched you?" I asked. "Yes that freak touched me!" "He touched my leg when I told him to get the hell away from me!" "That's why his stupid behind is drowning now!" A few of the older kids that were in the pool stood my man up and walked him to the edge. He had his hat in one hand and his empty glass in the other. While he was attempting to climb over the edge to get out, I went and stood in front of him. "My man, you touched my woman's leg?" I asked. "I didn't know she was your woman," he said with water drippin' from that stupid look on his face. "So you didn't see her with me all night?" "yeah, I seeent her," (grammatically correct as this statement was) "so what about it?" he said boldly. By this time, a crowd stood around the pool. "Yo, who is this guy?" Kenny asked out loud looking around for answers. Nobody said a word. I guess it was all of three seconds later before pool boy felt a size 11 foot flush on the side of his face. I swear if we were in the Georgia Dome, it would have been a 65 yard field goal! All you heard was "Ohhhhhhhh" from the people that had crowded around, then a big splash, only this time, he didn't yell for help. Homeboy was O-U-T! Kenny jumped in to help get him out of the pool. "Baby, you didn't have to do that," Brianna said, "You see I had everything under control!" "I understand that hon, but how was I gonna stand here and let this dude not only disrespect me, but disrespect you as well? Sorry, but a man's gotta do what a mans gotta do." Kenny pulled this guy out of the pool with the assistance of a few other guys and laid him on the grass. Come to find out, he was a friend of someone that lived around the corner from Kenny, and from that back yard on the adjacent street you could see into Kenny's back yard plain as day, so he took it upon himself to invite himself over. Then he tries to get with my girl! "Yo man, help me wake this cat up so he can go back to wherever he came from," Kenny asked.

As he laid there on the grass, my girl Kennedy walked over to him, bent over and said…. "Dag, you got knocked the HECK out!" Everyone bust out laughing. I must admit, I was a little worried about him. I wasn't trying to catch a case, especially here in Georgia so yes, I had a vested interest in waking him up as well. After about three minutes of trying to revive him, he spit out a bit of water and began moving around. He was Ok! "Whew!" "Ok man, you gotta go now partner." Kenny escorted him out the back yard and pointed him in the direction in which he came. He was still drunk from that kick though. You could tell by the way he staggered back around the corner. He had the whole party watching him walk away.

"Jay, I love you baby, but I don't need you doing anything stupid like that again," Brianna tried to reason. *"I can handle myself! Trust me, as many guys try me, if I didn't know how to handle myself I would have BEEN a victim by now! I don't need you going to jail over some fool. We have too much to lose now baby." "I understand honey, and I apologize for reacting the way I did," I said.*
Deep down I knew that if the situation ever came up again, I would react the same way. No matter where I may be now in my life, I'm still from the projects. I love the Lord with all my heart and I am not trying purposely to go to jail, but as long as you don't harm me or mine we'll be fine. There is a certain line that can't be crossed.

"Now that you've ripped up my party fool, you and Brianna need to get over here on the card table and let's REALLY see how tough you two are," Kenny said. Everyone started laughing and we really enjoyed rest of the night.

The next day we took in a little more of Atlanta before it was time to leave and return back to Jersey. I really wasn't looking forward to leaving Atlanta. Who knows, maybe one day Brianna and I will make this our home!

Chapter 11

▼

The Offer

Two months had passed since our trip to Atlanta and the cold of Northern New Jersey was beginning to really settle in. Although I was born and raised here, I was pretty sick of the cold and snow. The older I got, the more I wanted out of Jersey. Brianna and I had talked about moving south, anywhere from Maryland to Georgia, but we never talked about when. One night while we were out at a jazz club, Brianna asked, "So when are we going to set the wedding date honey?" The question took me by surprise. Sure, we were engaged, but I never actually sat down and thought about WHEN I would become a husband. "I don't know hon, did you have a certain date in mind?" I asked, not really certain I was ready for the answer. Not that I didn't love her and want to marry her but truth is, I was Ok just knowing I was engaged to her "Well, I was thinking…what do you think about having our wedding on an island?" "Maybe Aruba, the Grand Caymans, or maybe even Jamaica?" Fact is, that sounded really good. This way, it doesn't have to be anything big and extravagant. We wouldn't have to invite a whole lot of people that we really don't want to be there AND we could have our honeymoon at the same time. "I think that's a great idea baby!" "Personally, I like Aruba, but Jamaica would be nice also," I said. "Fine, we will have our wedding in Aruba!" Brianna said as she jumped up and gave me a great big hug. "I'm getting married in Aruba…in Aruba…in Aruba." She was bouncing around the house singing the Aruba song now! I must admit, I was happy also. "Now, what about the date?" she asked.

"I was thinking next fall, maybe September or October," she said.
"Let's do it in October," I said as she was sitting up close to me just ready to give me a great big kiss no matter which month I said. "Baby! We're getting married next year!" her eyes began to swell up with tears. She gently touched my face as I kissed the inside of her hand. "I love you Mrs. McCallister" "I love you too Mr. McCallister" We began to kiss. "I'm getting maaaarried…. I'm getting maaaaaarried" She began to dance around the house again.

Next day at work, I was in my office when my boss came in and closed the door. I knew it had to be something serious because my boss NEVER came into my office. He was a big guy that didn't like to move around too much. Once he came in the office in the morning, he was usually stashed in his office until it was time for him to leave. If he didn't bring his lunch from home, he would either pick something up from anyone who was going out for lunch or he would order in. "Jay, I need to talk to you," he said. "Is everything Ok?" I asked, hoping I would still have my job after this conversation was over with. "Well, you know the company has had expansion plans in the works now for over two years and we have just completed construction on our North Carolina location. I was asked by the board who I felt would be the best individual to head that location and I chose you. You will be President and C.E.O of all Southeastern operations, and I wanted to be the first to congratulate you." I was speechless!

Not that I didn't think I could do the job, I just didn't know that my boss thought so highly of me. Besides, if I was to leave this location, a lot of the workload would be put on him until he found a replacement for me. No one there was qualified or had the knowledge to do what I did, so promot-

ing from within wasn't an option. "I really appreciate the opportunity Mr. Levin and it's something I will strongly consider. If you can please give me a few days to think it over I would really appreciate it." "Think it over?" he asked as if he was a little annoyed at my response. "What is there to think over? This is the opportunity of a lifetime, and the company has agreed to pay all of your expenses!" "Not only your moving expenses, but your day to day and your monthly expenses as well!" "Think it over?!" *He was right, this WAS the opportunity of a lifetime. As I stated earlier, I've been wanting out of Jersey anyway, AND the company is paying full boat for everything! What was there to consider? My family? My friends? Brianna? All of the above. My family and friends would understand. Besides, they would be able to come and visit me whenever they saw fit. It would give them the perfect opportunity to travel. Brianna was a whole different story. We had made plans. We've planned our future together and whatever affected me would affect her as well. I really didn't know how she would take the news. This kind of career move would put me well into six figures and keep in mind, I had just turned 30. This would be a major advancement in my career and could set us up for the rest of our lives. On the other hand, she had her own business. I wondered whether or not what she did could be done from another state, and if so, would SHE be Ok with leaving her family and friends as well. Boy this love thing...as beautiful as it is, can also be overwhelming.* "Just give me until the end of the week Mr. Levin. I promise I will have an answer for you by then," *I politely requested.* "Ok, but I'm warning you McCallister, don't blow this. This opportunity can set you up for the rest of your life." *Boy, didn't I know it!*

The first person I called was my mom and told her the good news. Needless to say, she was very happy for me and extremely proud. She really didn't want me to leave, but she totally understood the opportunity and tried her best to convince me that she was Ok with it, but I knew she would miss me. Of my siblings she and I were the closest and whenever she needed things done, from setting her alarm clock when daylight savings time would change, to taking her to the grocery store, it was me she would call. When I told her how much money I would be making, she was Ok with it FOR REAL! I would still be able to come home once or twice a month, plus I was going to buy her a car before I left. Yeah, she was Ok.

When I called Darryl, he was happier than I was! "You're moving to NC?!" "Really?" "NOW you're talking, and it's right on time. I had JUST met this sister from Charlotte on blackwomeninprison.com who said her release date is next month! I was trying my hardest to figure out a way to get out there and be there waiting for her right outside the gate when she got out now you come along and tell me that's where you're moving to!" "Yeah man, God is good isn't he?" he asked. I wasn't sure I wanted to co-sign that one, but God is definitely good. My children would be able to come and spend the summer with me. I know they would love to spend time away from Jersey as well, and having them with me in NC for the summers would be a good time for us to spend quality time together as well. Curt and T-mac would be cool with it, but Brianna could make or break the deal. We had planned to go out to dinner the next night because she had to work this night and I did not want to tell her over the phone, so I had a night to think about how I was going to tell her this. I needed it.

The next night came and Brianna was at my house by the time I got off. I walked in and she was sitting on my sofa eating a cup of yogurt watching the Oprah show that she had taped from the day before. "Hey baby!" she said as I walked thru the door. "Hi honey, how was your day?" sounding as exhausted as I felt. "My day was great! Come, sit down, I have something to show you. She pulled out this book of wedding invitations. "I was going to begin preparing the invitations to be sent out and I wanted us to decide together which ones would be best." I really was in no mood to be going thru wedding invitations, but Brianna seemed so eager to do this that I just went along with it. I really wanted to talk to her about my offer before we went out to eat, but I guess it will be wedding invitations for now. After about forty minutes of looking at what seemed like thousands of invitations, we decided on one set and were finally able to close the book. I changed clothes and we were off to the restaurant. All the way there, Brianna had this permanent smile on her face. We didn't say much to each other. I could tell she had the wedding on her mind.

The restaurant was so crowded that we had a 45 minute wait for a table, so I asked Brianna if we could sit at the bar. This was a strange request being that neither of us drank. She soon picked up that there was something on my mind. "What's the matter baby?" "It seems like something's been on your mind since you came home. Is everything Ok? Not sure where to begin. "Yeah baby, everything is fine," I tried to brush it off. "No it isn't Jay, I know you and you are not usually this quiet. Something is going on and I'm here baby, I'm here for you if you can just talk to me and tell me what it is." That was the beauty in Brianna. I knew that I can talk to her about anything and even if it was something she didn't like, there would not be a nasty or evil word out of her mouth. I just didn't want to disappoint her. "Brianna, the truth is yes, I do have something I need to talk to you about. All I ask is that you look at this in every way possible and try and see the benefits. "You're beginning to scare me Jay. Please tell me what it is," she begged.

"Well, today Mr. Levin came into my office...." "Oh my God Jay, you were fired?" "No baby, hear me out. He came into my office, sat down, and actually told me he had recommended me for a promotion." "Baby, that's great! Why do you seem so sad?" "Brianna the promotion calls for me to relocate to Charlotte. He recommended me to become President and C.E.O. of our new Southeastern operations." She looked at me and took my hand. "That is wonderful baby! I am so proud of you! For him to recognize you in that capacity speaks volumes for your value to the company. What did you tell him?" she asked. "I told him that I would think about it and get back to him by the end of the week. Baby this is an opportunity of a lifetime, but I cannot make this decision alone. You are a part of me now. You are a part of my life, a part of my future and whatever I decide we are going to have to decide together." Her face saddened. "What do you want *me to say baby? I can't tell you not to take this opportunity. That would be selfish of me and I love you way too much to take something like this away from you Jay." "Say you'll come with me," I blurted out. "Baby you know how much I love you and I will do ANYTHING for you, but right now is a bad time for me to make a move like that. I can't just walk away from what I do for a living. As bad as I want out of Jersey too, I can't just drop everything and leave. I have to plan for that. I have people that depend on me that I cannot just leave hanging."*

"You must understand that I would never choose work over you, but other people's lives depend on me also. As much as I want to be selfish about this, I can't be. I really hope you can understand that," she pleaded. "Well what are you saying Bri?" "Baby I'm saying that you are going to have to go on without me. Give me two, three months maybe and I will be there with you, but I just cannot up and leave." All of a sudden I didn't have an appetite anymore. I wanted to just curl up in a ball and roll the hell out of there. I felt...well, I don't know how I felt, but it wasn't good. I totally understood what Brianna was saying, but what was I gonna do in Charlotte for three months without her? She saw the disappointment in my face. "Baby I love you more than I have ever loved any man in my life and I am still going to be your wife next year. Never forget that. Nothing is going to change that Jay. What you are going there to do is going to provide a lifetime of success for US and I have to respect that, and as much as I am going to hate being without you, I know that God will not keep us apart for long. He brought us together Jay and look at us, we are making plans to get married next year! That is a blessing. You being offered this position is a blessing! We just have to recognize this for what it is and thank him for once again blessing us in only a way that he can." I felt better after Brianna gave me that reassurance, but you don't understand, she has become such a part of me that every time I breathe, I smell her...everywhere I look I see her face. Just thinking about not having her there when I come home or not being able to put my key in her door after a long hard days work is going to be miserable. Besides, I know absolutely no one in Charlotte. I don't know

what kind of test God is putting me through now, but I was not ready for it. Regardless of how I felt, I knew this was something I had to do.

Brianna and I had dinner and went back to her place and made love till the sun came up. That next morning, I came to grips with the situation. I was leaving for Charlotte and she wasn't coming with me!

CHAPTER 12

▼

CHARLOTTE, NORTH CAROLINA

About a week before I was to leave to North Carolina for good, Darryl, T. and myself flew to Charlotte for a few days so that I could find a place to call home. I had contacted a real estate broker there to show us around. Brianna couldn't go because she had to work that weekend, but she promised she would make the move with me the following weekend and leave to fly back to Jersey that Sunday night. Charlotte was up and coming. Many people called it the 'new Atlanta' simply because so many black folk were beginning to migrate there as well. That is what Atlanta was known for…transplants. From single women escaping bad relationships to Northerners wanting a better, less expensive life—the South seemed to be the place to go. There were so many businesses choosing Charlotte to break ground that within a year, it would be just as big and probably as heavily saturated with people from other states as Atlanta.

When we arrived, It was a bright and sunny Saturday. We would only be in town until Tuesday morning, so we had a lot to do between the time we arrived and Tuesday. We rented a car, checked into our rooms at the Mar-

riott and set about making our way around Charlotte. We drove thru Center City, East Charlotte, North Charlotte, Lake Norman and South Charlotte before deciding Center City would be the best location for me to settle in, at least while I was by myself. Once Brianna and I got married, maybe had a child or two, then moving to a suburb would be the thing to do, but being in the heart of a the city was the place to be. That is where my company's new location would be also, so it only made sense.

C-City is where everything was happening. Like Manhattan in N.Y. and Downtown Atlanta in Atlanta, C-City was the spot. There was theatre, many five-star restaurants, the Charlotte Symphony, and the Performing Arts Center. We met with the real estate agent later on that afternoon and after driving around for a couple of hours looking at different places, I settled on a nice spacious loft right in the heart of downtown Charlotte. It was definitely a bachelor pad. It seemed to once be a factory that was converted into lofts. Man was it huge! Sky lights lit the vaulted ceilings all around the top level. Oh, it had 5 levels which included 4 bedrooms and 3 bathrooms. On the fenced in roof was my private terrace complete with Jacuzzi. There was also an indoor glass elevator. Yeah, I was living large and I am certain Brianna would love it also! I couldn't wait for her to see it! "When I get home I am selling everything I have and I should be back in a couple of weeks after you move in," Darryl said. "No way can I go back to Jersey and be Ok with where I live now after seeing this!" "Yeah man, this is crazy," T. chipped in. "This is what you call living!" "You've definitely come up my brother, I'm proud of you!" I signed the paperwork from the real estate agent, wrote him a check and he gave me the key. He also stated that he would take care of having all of my utilities turned on within a few days. It was a done deal. I was now a resident of Charlotte, North Carolina.

We hung out that night at a local club. "Man, look at all the honeys in here!" Darryl said. He was right, Charlotte was boomin' with sisters from all over!

T. and I mostly chilled but Darryl met this young lady named Denise that happened to be with a few girlfriends. They came over to where we were sitting and decided to join us. Darryl looked as if he had just found Jesus! Denise was very attractive, seemed to have it all together AND didn't have a prison record! "Hey Denise, these are my boys Jay and T-Mac…fellas, this is Denise and her girlfriends Michelle and Zora." We exchanged pleasantries and they all sat down. "So, you fellas are from New Jersey huh?" Zora asked. "Yeah, my boy Jay here is a big executive of his company and they've just finished building a location here in Charlotte, so he's relocating here to run their Southeastern operations," Darryl said proudly. "Wow, I'm impressed!" said Zora. Zora was about 5'6" very attractive and shaped like a coca-cola bottle…thick in the hips, slim waist and boomin' up top. Yeah, she was VERY shapely, as a lot of these southern women are. "Why don't we dance Jay?" she politely asked. "Cool"

We hit the dance floor. From the corner of my eye I could see Darryl and Denise on one side and T. and Michelle on the other side. Everyone was dancing and having a good time. "THIS is the way life should be," I thought to myself. The only thing missing was Bri. After a few dances, Zora and I sat down. "So tell me Jay-a young, successful, handsome brother like you MUST have a woman somewhere. I know those Jersey women couldn't be that foolish to allow someone such as yourself to be out there all alone?" she asked. "As a matter of fact, I am engaged to be married Zora. My fiancée's name is Brianna and she's still in Jersey. She's not going to be able to move here for a few months, however, we should still find time once in a while to spend with each other. It may be difficult, but we'll manage." She seemed a little disappointed, but she was very respectful. "It seems that all the good men are always taken. I would never do anything to disrespect another woman because I would not want to be disrespected myself, but there's nothing wrong with being friends is there?" "Of course not," I said. I don't see anything at all wrong with that." "So, are you all moved in?" she asked. No, I won't officially be here until next weekend. We're here this weekend so I could pick out a place to live and learn a little about the area." "What area are you looking to move?" she asked. "Actually, I have *already signed a lease at Cartier Estates" "Really!? What unit?" I don't know about units, but my address is 1117 #7." "Well, that would make us neighbors then wouldn't it?" she said rather happily. Afraid to ask "What, what uh, what do you mean neighbors?" "I am in Unit 1116 #9!" "Ok, then I guess we WILL be neighbors huh?!" I reached out to shake her hand. She held it for a second then gave me a card. "Here, take my number. This way you can call me when you get back in town. When are you guys leaving," she asked. "Tuesday morning. I'm going to need to find furniture and all, and I planned on doing that all day Monday." "Boy, how lucky are you?" she said with a big smile on her face. "Monday's happen to be my day off, and since I definitely know where all the good furniture stores are, I'll be happy to show you and your friends around…if It's Ok with your fiancée. By the way, what's her name again," she asked. "Brianna, and I'm sure she wouldn't mind." See, Brianna and I didn't have those types of trust issues. She trusts me and I trust her. I'm sure once I tell her about Zora, she will not have a problem with it at all. "Ok so Monday it is," I said to her. Darryl and his new friend had just come back from the dance floor and seemed to really be hitting it off. T.-and Michelle barely spoke. T. was quiet anyway. He was like a bodyguard, always on the lookout for trouble. Women other than Blink really didn't interest him.*

The next day, Darryl had plans to hook up with Denise, and T. and I was going to check out what Churches were in the area. After all, I had to find a new church home now.

It was around 9am this beautiful Sunday morning. Charlotte was a very pretty place. Lots of trees, lots of greenery. The first thing I did was call Brianna. "Hello" "Good morning baby!" I said. "Hey sweetheart!" "I was hoping you called me before I left for church and I was just on my way out. So, how are things going in Charlotte?" "A lot better than expected," I told her. "I've found the hottest place for us sweetie!" And I began to tell her all about it. "That sounds sooooo nice baby! I can't wait to get there!" "When are you guys coming back home?" "Tuesday morning our flight leaves. We should be in Newark Airport by 11:30 am," "Ok, I can pick you up. I miss you Jay." "I miss you too Bri." "Where's Darryl and T-mac," she asked. "T. and I are about to go out and see what type of churches are in the area and Darryl's out with Denise, this young lady he met last night at this club we went to." "Denise? Club? So you were out partying last night huh? Remember what happened the last time you and Darryl went out to a club together don't you?" she asked. "Yeah, I fell in love!" "Good thing I don't have to go thru that again huh honey?" I asked, trying to sound as innocent as possible. "So Darryl met some woman last night at the club...and what about you? I know those country women love themselves some up North brothers, so how many were up in YOUR face Jay?" She wasn't upset, actually she had a joking tone, but I was not sure whether or not I should tell her about Zora. This was another test. Could I be honest enough to tell her that I met another woman that I just so happen to be neighbors with that's beautiful, has no man, no children, and really trying to get at me? Oh, by the way, she gave me her number also and we're going furniture shopping tomorrow! "Baby.... (I guess you know that when a brother starts out a conversation by saying 'baby', a lie is about to follow).... T. and I were just chillin' all night. It wasn't even like that. I smiled, said hi to a few ladies, but that's it." (Hey, I never said I was perfect. This love thing aint easy! I never made it a habit of lying to Brianna, but this kinda caught me off guard.) "Um hum," she said. "Ok baby, I'm going to be late for church. I will be home all afternoon. Call me later Ok?" "Of course I will my love. Be careful and say a prayer for me." "I always do!"

After driving around for a few hours, T. and I hooked up with Darryl. He and Denise were at an outside eatery sippin' on Mamosa and kickin' it like they had known each other for year. "Jay...T...what's up fellas?" "Denise has been showing me around. It's NICE out here!" "I'm seriously thinking about moving down here myself," he said. Denise had a big smile on her face. T. and I knew that Darryl was NOT leaving his mom and sick dad up North to move down here. "Whatever man," T. said. "Seriously, you'll see." "Yo Jay, let me talk to you for a minute." "Listen man, I wasn't planning on hookin' up with somebody when we got here and I only brought but so much money. Can you please let me hold something until we get home?" Typical Darryl. How are you gonna meet someone and can't afford to take her out? "There's a jazz concert in the park later on and Denise and I are going to check it out." "Man, I thought you came here with US?" I asked. "You aint never gonna see this woman again after Monday, so why go thru all this?" "Why do you think?" "Come on man, just because you have Brianna in your life now and you are TRYIN' to do the right thing, don't act like you don't know! I got plans for that tonight," he said making reference to Denise. "You know I gotta give her the goodness before I leave!" "She wants it just as much as I do, and I'm just the man to give it to her!" "You're a fool man...here" I pulled out my wallet and gave him $100 bill. "Don't spend it all in one place. You're on your own after that." "Let's get out of here T. Nice to see you again Denise. Take care of my man." "Darryl is in good hands, trust me" she smiled. So did he!

The next morning I got up early and called Zora. (Hello) "Hey Zora, this is Jay, remember me?" "Jay who?" she said. "I'm just kidding. Of course I remember you. How are you?" "I'm cool. Listen, are you still going to be able to show me a few furniture stores today?" I asked. "I would never tell you something that I wouldn't do. I guess you don't know me well enough yet to know that. What time will you be ready," she asked. "Whenever's best for you," I politely said "I've already been up and out jogging, so I am ready now if you are. It's probably better if we get an early start anyway. Have you had breakfast yet," she asked. "Not yet, but I'm not hungry yet anyway. I'd just rather get started on the task at hand and we can grab something later if that's Ok with you," I told her. "Ok, why don't you come on over and we can leave from here," she said. "Ok, give me about 15 minutes." "Do you remember the address? I'm right in the next building to your left." "Yeah, I remember. See you in a few."

I went and knocked on T. and Darryl's door. "Who is it?" "It's me T., are you and Darryl ready to go check out some furniture with me and Zora."

"Man, Darryl ain't even here. He called me last night and told me he was over Denise's and he would see us today, and I'm still asleep." "Hit me when you get back. I'll be here, probably still sleep." "Cool," I said. Obviously, whatever Darryl had planned for Denise worked. I just hope he's careful out here. (doorbell)

"Come on in, the door is open." I walked in Zora's house and it was laid out! It was built the exact same as mine only she had a lot of 'stuff'. That is the only way I can describe it…stuff! Mainly exotic statues and paintings. She also had pictures of herself, big poster size pictures hanging up in different places, of her posing…in the nude! And the statues, they were of body parts, really exotic and arousing. "Wow, your place is nice Zora. Are you a model?" I called out to her upstairs. "You can say that. I teach art class in my spare time. NUDE art!" "Well Ok," trying my best not to look at the pictures. It would be embarrassing if she came downstairs and saw certain things saying Hi besides my hand! She made her way downstairs in some spandex shorts and a belly tank top. "Isn't it a little chilly for that?" I asked. It was cold up North, but just a little chill in the air down here. "This is what I jog in. I hope you don't mind if I wear this. I really don't feel like changing," she said apologetically. "It's cool. If you're Ok, I'm Ok"…Boy do I love Brianna…Boy do I love Brianna…Boy do I love Brianna…. I had to keep telling myself that. "Come on let's go," she said. She led the way of course. I may be in love, but I'm still a man and if you can just close your eyes for a second and imagine what I saw walking in front of me, you would understand why everywhere we went that morning…she led! I think it's disrespectful to stare at another woman when you are with YOUR woman but women, I don't care what your man tells you, there's not a man alive that would turn his head if a beautiful woman with a body like a goddess walked in front of him. "So, what price range are you looking in so I will know where to begin" "I don't know, just take me where you would go if it were you picking out furniture for yourself." From the looks of her place, Zora had really nice taste in furniture. Yeah she was a little freaky, but her furniture was nice.

After going to three different stores, we finally found a place that I liked. I picked out a living room set, kitchen set, and two bedroom sets. The only one left to pick out was the master bedroom set. "Look Jay, this one is nice." She called me over to a set and it was tight! I loved it! It was an 8-piece set, with a very unusual style. It was marble. The foot board, headboard and the posts which were shaped like Roman columns and all made of marble. It had a two-step foot stool to get into the bed which sat high off the floor. If you rolled off the bed, you would definitely have a concussion if you didn't have carpet in your bedroom. "Ohhh, this mattress feels soooooooo good," she said. "Come here, try it out." She pulled me back on the bed as I swung my legs around to lie fully on top(of the bed). She was lying next to me. I turned over and we were face to face. Then she turned her back to me and then turned again to lie on her stomach.

I caught myself when this guy walked by and said, "Damn," when he saw her. I didn't have any business laying in that bed with her, not even to 'test drive' it. I jumped up. "So, how do you like it?" she asked. "Yeah, yeah, it's cool" "Where's the sales guy, let me get the heck out of here," I said to myself. After paying for everything, the manager promised to have it delivered and set up by Wednesday. I would give Zora my key and she would be there to make sure everything went right.

After going to pick out appliances, we stopped and got something to eat. "I really want to thank you Zora." "I don't know how I would have gotten all this done in one day if it weren't for you! You're a lifesaver!" "Don't sweat it Jay. You seem to be a really nice guy and someone I would love to have as a friend. Your woman is so lucky! What's her name again?" "Just kidding! Brianna is lucky to have a guy like you. See, women like me only have 'friends' like you, never you." "What is wrong with the brothers out here?!" I asked. "As beautiful and sweet as you are how the heck can you be alone out here? I really cannot understand that." "The last relationship I had, I caught my man having sex in the back of his car in the lot behind his job after work one night. That was 2 years ago. Sorry, but I'm just not that trusting anymore. If I even SMELL the scent of D-O-G in a man, I'm gone. It seems to be that's all there is out here. Good, married men or DOGS! I've even considered going to the 'other race' thinking maybe a white man will treat me better, but honey as freaky as I am I know for a fact no white man can keep up with me. Makes me wonder sometime why my man had to sneak around and have sex with other women. My sex drive is waaaaay higher than the average woman's and I know I definitely held up MY part of the deal." "When it gets to that point Zora it's called GREED!" I said. "There's a LOT of brothers out here that can have a woman like you, a sexual goddess, and STILL have to have more. It's variety they seek. It's nothing against you at all. You just got caught up in it. A man like that will NEVER be faithful because his lust for newer and better will always remain his primary focus. It's like every year waiting for the newer model car to come out. You test drive it, take it around the block a few times then realize it's no better than the one you have at home, besides, the one at home is cheaper! But it doesn't stop you from searching." She tried to make logic of what I had told her, and I think she totally understood, but it seemed like the more I spoke the deeper into my eyes she was going. Like she was captivated by every word I spoke. I don't know if it was what I was saying or how my lips were moving when I said it, but I had to cut that conversation short. Boy do I love Brianna....

Tuesday morning came, Darryl came back to the hotel around 6am and knocked on my door. "Yo Jay, what time are we leaving?" "In a few hours man, leave me alone, I'm sleep." "Whatever man, come across the hall when you wake up," he yelled. By 8:30 we had dropped off the rent-a-car and was at the airport waiting for our flight. "Jay, Charlotte is ALL THAT man, I can't believe you are going to be living here!" Darryl said. "Yeah, it is nice out here. You're blessed my brother," chipped in T. 'Yeah, but I guess I'm still going to miss Jersey but I'll get over it," we laughed. By now I was really missing Brianna and couldn't wait to get back to Jersey to be with her. With all that's going on here in Charlotte, I mean with the new place, new position, and Zora as a neighbor—I would still decline the position if Brianna told me that she couldn't EVER move out here with me. I knew it would only be temporary and I guess I could deal with that....I hope!

CHAPTER 13

▼

GARDEN STATE GOODBYE

By the time we got back to Jersey, I was really beat. All I wanted to do was see Brianna. After being around Zora this past weekend, I was ready to fulfill some fantasies that only Brianna could fill. See, that's the thing about men. We can see all the booty we want to see out in the streets, but if we have a woman at home that's making love to us the way we want to be made love to, then it's nothing but something to look at. Just like guys who frequent strip clubs. It's not always about trying to sleep with the first dancer that pays a little us a little attention (not that I frequent strip clubs), nor is it about the $100 wasted on lap dances. That's just getting us ready for our woman when we get home, if we can manage to wake her up. So ladies, let me let you in on a little secret. If your man likes to 'hang out' and you like to get freaky but he's always gone, don't get upset. One night when he's just about to leave—say, "here honey, why don't you take this and you and a few of the fellas go to the strip club," and give him $100. Now all you gotta do is sit back, watch a movie, take a nap and by the time he gets in all nice and wound up, guess who is going to reap the benefits? See, I had thoughts of Zora when we were together. Not thoughts of cheat-

ing on Brianna and sleeping with Zora, but just wondering what it would be like if I did. That only made me want Brianna more! The only guys that take it to that next level and just HAVE to sleep with everything they come across are the one's that are simply greedy. Those are the one's you have to be careful of, because they could be carrying a little of everything in that magic stick!

The airport was packed and I was looking around for Brianna like a kid looking for a lost parent. "Hey baby, over here" I heard her say. "Yo there she is," said Darryl in a disgusted tone. Darryl was still upset because he had to leave Denise. As soon as we entered each other's space, Brianna and I couldn't wait to lock lips. "I missed you baby," she said. "I missed you too Bri" "Man, can we go. I gotta get home and make a phone call," Darryl snapped. "Hurry up and let me get this boy home," I said.

After dropping off Darryl and T., Briana and I went to my house. "So, did you really like Charlotte baby?" Brianna asked. "I love it! And I really think you will love it also." "It sounds beautiful and I can't wait to get there baby, but are you 100% certain that this is something YOU want to do? Forget about how I feel or what Mr. Levin expects of you, what about Jay? Is this what Jay wants?" "Brianna, you and I have spoken about getting out of Jersey many times, and now is the perfect opportunity. Charlotte is a lovely city filled with respectable black people. It's a very friendly place and definitely someplace I could see us settling in to." "Ok baby, I just want to make sure. I'm so happy for you!" she gave me a big hug. It felt so good to have a woman who understands that when there's opportunity there for her man to fulfill his dream of success, that she is behind him 110%. "So you will be coming with me next weekend when I actually move in right?" "Of course," she said. "I'll just leave to return home on Sunday. I know I'm going to miss you when I'm not there with you." She said. You will be out there all alone until the next time I will be able to come for the weekend." "I hate even thinking about it." I dare don't tell her that I wont be ALL alone, I mean with Zora living so close and us establishing a friendship. It's *not like I'm cheating on her or anything, but something about it just doesn't seem right. I know she has male friends and I have never made a big deal about it, and its not like she will never know about Zora, I just didn't feel then was the right time to talk about it. With women, you have to pick and choose the right time to bring certain things up. Although Brianna and I never had any major disagreements or arguments, she's still a woman and women by nature are emotional creatures. "I'm sure I'll be Ok Bri, honestly. No need to worry, but I will miss you terribly!" "I'm definitely going to miss this big head laying on my chest at night! Maybe I'll get a watermelon or something and lie it my chest in your place!" "Forget you! That watermelon can't rub your belly like you like," she said. "uhm, you got a point there." "That watermelon can't kiss you on your chest like this." (kissing slowly and gently) "Ok, another point well taken!" "It can't kiss you here...." I guess you know how we spent the rest of the night...and it wasn't talking about watermelons!*

The next few days at work were hectic. I had to bring Mr. Levin up to date on everything that was going on. The things that he never wanted to know, now he had to know. It would take him a while to find a replacement for me, so he would be taking on a whole workload and he needed to be brought up to speed in three days. Besides work, I only had three days to make my rounds to all of my family and friends and wish everyone well and let them know of my good fortune. I also wanted to give everyone an open invitation to come to Charlotte whenever they have an opportunity and I would be more than happy to host and entertain. Moving six hundred miles away definitely would not enable people to just "drop by" and in a way, that was a good thing. You're gonna have to CALL me and make PLANS to come see ME! No... "I was just in the neighborhood." Naw, that can't happen.

The next night, with me relocating and hoping never to have to move back to Jersey, an emergency meeting was necessary. I got the call from Curt at work that morning and even though I wanted to spend my last few nights in town with Bri, it was only right that me and the fellas hook up ONE of those night, and Wednesday night was better than any. Everyone met at my house. "I can't believe ya'll fools went to Charlotte without me!" Curt said. "T. told me it was off the chain down there…women EVERYWHERE!" I looked at T. as if to say, "why did you tell this man that—knowing that a city full of new women to him is like Asian tourists in Times Square…camera's, video recorders and all. "Charlotte is the spot Curt," Darryl stood up. "Our first night in town, I hooked up with a honey and we spent ALL WEEKEND together," like he had just spent the weekend with Jennifer Lopez! "This fool was out there like he LIVED in Charlotte," said T. "What about you Jay, I hear you didn't do so bad yourself?" "I don't know what you heard my brother, but I was cool." "Oh really, how is Zora?" "Man T., what else did you tell?" I asked. "So what's really going on Jay? I know Brianna is not moving to Charlotte with you and now you go down there and meet someone who lives so close to you that she can just walk over your house AND ya'll spend the day together?" "Did you tell Brianna about her?" "Brianna knows all about her" "YOU LYIN!" shouted Darryl. "You know you didn't tell Brianna about Zora!" "If you did, what did she say?" "Ok, let's keep it real. No I didn't tell Brianna about Zora, not yet anyway but I am." "When?" said Curt. "Before or after you sleep with her?" "Zora and I are just friends. I met her the night Darryl met his friend. She just so happens to live next door to me, but she's cool. She understands I have a woman…a fiancee, and she is cool with that. There's limits and she is not trying to disrespect Bri." "By the way, she's a nude art instructor!" "What!" said Darryl. "She told you that?" "The morning we went to pick out furniture, I went to her house and she had these paintings up" "of her?" T. asked. "No of her mother, what do you think? Yes, of her!" "Yo, that's crazy," said Curt. "I don't know how all of a sudden you've become this changed man and will be able to ignore a nude artist living right next door to you!" "Did you and Brianna set a wedding date yet?" T. asked. "Yeah, we're getting married next October in Aruba." "Cool" "Yeah that's cool and all, but next October is a long time away," Darryl said. "A lot can happen between now and then." My boys still didn't believe in me. They knew I cared for Brianna, but they really didn't believe how much. Yeah, the temptation of Zora was going to be a lot for me to deal with. Sorta like putting a recovering alcoholic in a liquor store to work. Fact is, when WAS I going to tell Brianna about Zora? When she got there? Then, all of a sudden…"oh yeah honey, this is my next door neighbor!" "Well I really wish you the best out there in Charlotte," Curt said. "Don't worry, while you're gone, we'll keep an eye on Brianna for you. "I know she has all kinds of guys jockin' her and with you out of the picture…" "Oh, so now I should have to worry about Brianna huh?" "Why should you? She don't have to worry about you does she?" Curt was being sarcastic. I have never had to worry about Brianna cheating on me. It was never a thought. Since we met, we've been inseparable so why should I have to worry about her now? Maybe it was ME I didn't trust. Curt had planted a seed that I hadn't had to think about before. I WILL be gone. I won't be at Bri's when she gets home, and she won't be at my house when I get home from work. I wonder are we at least gonna talk everyday? What Brianna and I have is special, and I really didn't want that to change. I really wish she was moving with me now instead of in a few months. I don't believe God brought us together for it to end because of me relocating for the benefit of us both.

The rest of the night we all just sat around, reminisced and cracked jokes. I'm really going to miss my boys.

Later on that night, Brianna came over to spend the night with me. I'm glad she did because I really wanted to talk to her. Curt's words earlier that night had me feeling a little insecure and I just needed to be sure about a few things. "Brianna, you know I love you and I know you love me. We are engaged and our wedding date is set. Since you and I met, we have been together practically every day. Now that I am moving, do you think this is going to change the way you feel about me?" "What kind of question is that Jay?" She only calls me by my name when she's not too happy with me. "What makes you all of a sudden think that I am going to change my feel-

ings for you just because I won't see you every night? If anything, it will only make me miss you more." "Do you plan on changing your feelings for me?" she asked. "Of course not!" "My feelings for you will never change Brianna. I'm in this for the duration." "I just want you to know that you can always trust me. No matter how far I am away from you, you will always be with me." I truly believe Brianna and I will be fine. It is going to take getting used to I suppose. I mean, not having her around me all the time.

The next few days were split between work, my children, my mom and Brianna.

Finally the day came and it was time to leave. I can't say yet that I am going to miss New Jersey, but I do know that I am ready to begin my new life in Charlotte.

Chapter 14

Trouble in Paradise

All of my furniture was shipped earlier in the week, and my clothes were shipped by courier two days earlier. The only thing I had to take with us on the plane was a few pieces of luggage that had enough clothes to last me for a week. Brianna had a bag for the weekend. It was finally Saturday morning and our flight was to leave early that afternoon. Darryl and T. took us to the airport. We parked in the garage under the airport and proceeded to take the elevator to the main terminal. As the elevator door opened, a tall light-skinned man in a blue suit was about to step in. As he walked by us he stopped, "hey miss, don't I know you from somewhere?" he asked looking at Brianna. "Excuse me but I don't think so," Brianna said. "One thing I don't forget is a face, especially one as pretty as yours! It would be impossible for me to forget you!" Now I'm standing there listening to this dude flirt with my woman, but I am interested in seeing where this is going, so I continue to listen. "I've seen you in a club or somewhere like that, as a matter of fact, I was talking to you. I just can't remember your name. You really don't remember me?" he asked Brianna. "Sir I have never seen you before in my life," Brianna insisted. "Hon, maybe it was at the Crystal Palace," I chipped in. "That's it—the Crystal Palace," the man said. "You don't know me?!" Now Brianna was getting upset. "Come on honey, I really don't have time for this." She stepped off the elevator and began walking toward the terminal. Darryl, T. and myself were still standing there.

"Take care," the stranger said as the elevator door closed. By the time we caught up to Brianna, she was on her way thru the security checkpoint. "Why did you react the way you did?" I asked. "Is there something I need to know?" She was so upset she kept walking toward the gates. Darryl and T. could not go past the checkpoint, so I had to say my goodbyes to them there. "You cool man?" Darryl asked. "Yeah, I'm cool" really I was more confused than ever. Who was this dude? Why was my woman so upset because he said he knew her? What was the Crystal Palace REALLY all about? I was determined to get some answers over the next few days that's for sure, beginning with this plane ride. "Don't worry man, we'll keep an eye on Brianna for you," T. said. "I'm sure it's no biggie. Don't let it stress you." "Aiight fellas.... I'm out!" "Be easy and hold it down for me." "Jay, if you see Denise, tell her I'll be back out there towards the end of the month. Tell her I miss her!" "Aiight playa. I'll call you when I get to NC."

I caught up to Brianna who was sitting by our departure gate. You could tell she was really upset. She had already checked in and everything. I sat my carry on next to her and went to check in. After getting my boarding pass, I sat down next to her. "So, you want to explain to me what the hell that was all about?" "There's nothing to explain," she said. "I'll tell you like I told him, I have no idea who that man was and I have never seen him before in my life." "So, this man who doesn't even know your name just happens to know you work at the Crystal Palace and you're telling me he's lying?...that you've never even spoken to him?" I asked. "Listen, I'm not saying he didn't see me at the Palace, but he acted like I was all up in his face or something, and that definitely is not the case." "I just don't understand why that would upset you so much. I want you to tell me exactly what goes on there!" "What kind of 'club' is the Crystal Palace?" "Why are you taking me through all this?" she asks hysterically. "I already told you Jay, it is a club...a DANCE club! People perform there, that's it!" "People *like who, musical artists? unknown people? Do they dance, sing, act, tell jokes…what is it?" "It's a regular club Jay, that's it!" "Well guess what, the next time I'm back on town, I'll come visit you there!" She didn't seem too happy about that. "I can't believe that after all this time, you don't trust me!" "All the time we've shared, the plans we've made…going to church, worshiping together, making wedding plans, I really can't believe that because of this…this…person, that you can sit here and really act like I am lying to you!" "Do you trust me Jay?" she asked bluntly. "Of course I trust you Brianna, but all the time you and I have been together, I have never made it a big deal what type of work you do for a living, but when I have men stopping my woman in the streets and a conversation takes place like the one you and ole boy just had, one can only wonder. Come on, seriously, what if it were me?" "I have been more than understanding about your profession, late hours and all, but now you have the nerve to act like I don't have any rights asking any questions concerning what just took place!" "What exactly is YOUR role at the Crystal Palace? What part do YOU play? "You just can't leave it alone can you?" she broke down and began to cry. "Maybe I should just go back home. I really want to come with you, but if it's going to be a weekend full of questions, I really would rather not even come now." I was seriously considering waiting until the next day to leave, just so I could go to the Palace. Now my curiosity was at an all time high. "Just because I am asking you questions about what exactly you do, you decide you don't want to come to Charlotte with me?" "If that's how you really feel, then maybe it WOULD be better if you went back home." She stood up and went back over to the airline agent at the counter by the gate, said a few things, came back over to me and picked up her bag and told me that she would catch a taxi home. I'm not gonna front, I was hurt. I really wanted to show Brianna the new place because I knew she would flip over it. I also had missed her and just wanted to be with her this weekend, but was I really wrong to ask questions, especially with what had just taken place? As much as I wanted to, I didn't stop her. I don't know what it was that was causing Brianna to act this way. Was it me relocating and she just really didn't want to tell me that she was really upset? Or was whatever it was she did for a living really that important to her that it would cause her to react in such a way? Whatever the case, I was on my way to Charlotte.... Alone!*

Any other time I had a problem with a woman, it wouldn't really bother me simply because of one or two reasons; One, because I wouldn't allow myself to become that attached emotionally that if something happened it wouldn't bother me and two, I would most likely always have someone else anyway. This was different. I wasn't prepared for this. Even though I truly loved Brianna with all my heart, the first thing I did when I got to Charlotte airport was call Zora to see if she would be available to pick me up, but I got her answering machine. I left her a message and told her that I was back in town and for her to stop by when she had the opportunity. I had a limo service take me home. Calling mom and letting her know that I had made it safely was my number one priority. I knew she would be sitting by the phone waiting to hear from me. Funny, but when I would have problems with my women, I would always call my mom. Not to tell her about what was going on, because my mom was too nosey to let into my personal business like that, but just to talk to her. She was missing me already. "So you like it down there huh?" she asked. "Yeah, I really do. It is beautiful!" "Just let me know when you want to come down and I will send for you." "Oh you can believe that I WILL let you know and it wont be that long either. Where's Brianna, isn't she there with you?" Now she HAD to bring that up! "No, she had to stay in Jersey for another week. She'll be here next weekend." "What kind of work does she do again?" Maybe it WASN'T a good idea to call her! "You know what ma, let me call you back. I'm just getting in and I need to do a few things. I just wanted to let you know that I made it here safely." "Ok, tell Brianna I said hi when you talk to her." "I will make sure I do that!"

Next person I called was Darryl. I didn't bother getting into what happened between Brianna and I, hell he was there when it happened, but I did tell him that Brianna wasn't with me. "What! She didn't go with you!"

he said in a hushed tone. "Well, at least Zora will be happy! Have you called her yet?" *he asked.* "Yeah, I called her when I landed to see if she could pick me up, but she wasn't in." "Don't forget to tell Denise I'll be there in a few weeks. (doorbell)*—"Yo man, someone's at my door, let me call you back." "Cool" I knew it wasn't Brianna changing her mind, she didn't even know my address, so it could only be one person. I opened the door and Zora was standing there looking as good as ever.* "Hey you, I just got in and heard your message. Sorry I wasn't here to get your call. How long have you been in?" *I invited her in.* "I just got here about 40 minutes ago from the airport." "You as in JUST you? Where's Brianna, I'm really looking forward to meeting her?" "Brianna didn't come this weekend. Something came up in Jersey and she had to stay." *I could tell Zora wasn't TOO disappointed.* "Oh well, I guess I'll just have to wait to meet her." "Do you start working this coming week?" *she asked.* No, actually I don't start until the following week." "So what are you going to do all week?" "Get moved in I suppose. I still have a lot to do." "Well, if you need any help don't be shy about asking me. Would you like to grab something to eat later on?" "Sure why not," *I said.* "Ok, just call me when you're ready."

I really felt like calling Brianna, but I didn't want to seem weak. After all, it was HER who decided not to come. Whatever her reasons were, I don't think it was that bad that she could not have been here with her man. All because I was questioning her about her profession. After Zora left, I put away some of my clothes and laid down for what I thought was a few minutes but actually turned out to be more like two hours. When I woke up, I was really hungry. The first thing I thought about was Brianna, the second thing.... Zora (let me call her) "Hello" "Hey Zora, it's Jay. I was just wondering if you would be ready in an hour to go and grab some food?" "An hour will be fine. What have you been doing," *she asked.* "Nothing much. I put away my clothes, and went to sleep for a minute. That's it really, I just woke up." "What else do you have to do?" *she asked.* "Take a shower, shave and change my clothes." "Would you mind if I came over now? Denise was *just over here and now that she's gone, I'm kinda bored. I can wait and watch T.V. until you are ready." "Sure, why not!"*

A few minutes later the doorbell rang. "Come on in," I yelled out. She took the stairs to meet me on the third level, she wasn't too fond of the elevator. The third level is where my bedroom, two closets, a sitting room with a flat screen T.V. and the master bathroom were located. I hadn't set the T.V. into the wall yet, so it was just lying against the wall. "I won't be that much longer," I yelled out to her from the bathroom. "It's fine Jay, take your time. Is there anything I can do to help you?" she asked. "Actually there is, if you would look in my bedroom and take those clothes off of my bed and run an iron over them, I would really appreciate it. The iron is in the pantry on the 2nd level." "I guess I can do that for you. Just don't make it a habit. This is a job for your woman, and since I'm not that...." "Yeah, yeah, I know whatever Z." Zora was cool. Someone I could really chill with. Fact is, I really wanted to talk to someone about how I felt about Brianna. I did not want to discuss it too much with the fellas, because certain things you just don't discuss with your boys, besides I would have really preferred a woman's point of view and since I had cut off all my 'friends', Zora came along at just the right time. After she was done, she made her way back upstairs. "Here—what would you like me to do with your shirt?" "Oh you can just lay it back across the bed if you don't mind." She kinda caught me by surprise. All I had on was a pair of boxer briefs and some timberland boots, and was just about to slip on a tee shirt. "Excuse me, did I come too quick?" I don't really know which way she meant that, so I left it alone. "Sit down Zora, I want to talk to you about something," I asked. She sat on the edge of my bed "What's wrong Jay?" seems like you really have something on your mind. Is everything Ok? By the way your room is really nice!" I reached in my bag and pulled out a picture of Bri and I and sat it on my dresser. "Oh please can I see?" she begged. "She's a very attractive woman Jay! You make a beautiful couple. See, that's what I'm talking about…black love!"

I repeat, Zora was really cool, and I really felt it would be easy to talk to her. "Zora, what do you do for a living?" I asked. I'm an educator by day and as I told you, a nude art instructor part time. Why do ask?" "When you say an educator, exactly what does that mean?" I asked. "I teach 8th grade at the local middle school." "Now was that hard for you to tell me?" She looked at me with a puzzled look on her face. "Why don't you just tell me what happened," She asked. "Well, first off, let me tell you how long Brianna and I have been together and bring you up to date. See Brianna and I...." and I gave it to her just from the standpoint of me not knowing anything about what Brianna does, and about this strange dude from the airport. Zora listened to it all and basically told me that I was a fool for not being more inquisitive from the beginning. Let me explain why I didn't. The way I just asked Zora what she does for a living, it was no big deal. Generally, being that I am not in love nor am I trying to be in love (with her), how I talk and the things I say generally gives me a good indication on how I feel about person. I mean, I am not going to talk foul or disrespectful to a woman, but I will know what to say and what not to say. With most women, it's no big deal for me to ask questions. With Brianna, I didn't want her to think it was no big deal only because I was really feelin' her and didn't want to blow it by sounding jealous. No matter how many times the thought crossed my mind, I quickly got rid of it. I didn't want her to have any negatives thoughts about me at all. "Why does this guy ask so many questions?" I didn't want her in that frame of mind, but now it's a different story. I WANT to know! According to Zora, she believes something freaky is going on inside the 'Palace'. "From what you described to me, it could be any type of club. I'm just saying something doesn't seem right." "Maybe your next trip out there you should drop in and see for yourself," she proposed.

That sounded like an excellent plan.

Chapter 15

The Crystal Palace

I had spent most of the week doing things with Zora and getting my place together. I even went to the school where Zora taught. It was cool, but dealing with a bunch of horny 8th graders can be a challenge to ANY adult. It was now towards the end of the week. I had spoken to Brianna a few times, but not really about anything major. I didn't want to bring up the Palace again until I had the chance to really find out what it was about. I was due to begin work the coming week and I probably would not have the opportunity to go back to Jersey anytime soon.

As the weekend came, curiosity was getting the best of me. I wanted to know what goes on inside the Crystal Palace and I know the weekend was as good a time as any, but I couldn't leave. I thought to myself that maybe I can have someone I know go in there and see and simply let me know whether I really needed to be worried or not. Who can I ask that I can trust to tell me the truth, without making it sound any worse or any better than it really was. Darryl would have definitely embellished it either way. Either it would have been worse than it really was or not as bad as he would make it seem. I needed an honest assessment. Curt? Please, Curt would have been more concerned about the number of available women it would have been.

That basically left me with T-mac, which wasn't a bad choice at all. He would definitely give it to me honestly, but he wasn't really the type of person that would go to a club by himself and just hang-out. So I called another friend of mine. He wasn't really in our circle so to say, but he grew up with me from my high school days. He knew the fellas and they knew him. They were all cool. His name was Brian. Brian was the type of person that would go to a different club every weekend. Either a strip club or a regular club. He was divorced and determined not to settle down ever again. He was perfect to go along with T. I would not tell him the situation. I'd simply let him know that I have relocated, but my boy there was looking to hang out and since I wasn't there, would he fill in for me. Like I said, they knew each other anyway.

"Yo Brian! What's been up PATner?" "I know this ain't Jay-nice?" "Where you been fella?" "Man I'm down in Charlotte now. My company offered me a promotion and I just moved last weekend!" "Get out of here! Charlotte? I hear they got some poppin' clubs down there!" "I wouldn't know yet man, I haven't been here long enough. Me and the fellas went to one a few weeks ago. It was pretty hot!" "My boy Darryl hooked up with one sister. He can't WAIT to get back down here!" "Don't worry, give me till the end of the month…you'll see me!" he said. I got right to the point. "Listen, what are you doing tonight?" I asked. "I'm deciding right now which club I'm going to, but I don't know yet," he said. "Reason I ask is that my boy T-mac was tryin to go out tonight to, but the rest of the fellas got other things going on and his girl is leaving town for the weekend, so he asked me to holla at you and see if you wanna hang out tonight." "Yeah, yeah, that sounds kinda cool. Give him my number and tell him to call me." "Bet, I'll do that now and you two hook up later on." "Aaiiight" "Cool, call me next week," he said. "Will do"

Now I had to call T. Hell, I don't even know if he's available.

(phone ringing) "Hello" "T. What's up baby boy?" "Nothing much Jay, sittin' back watching the soaps I taped last week." Oh, I forgot to mention, T. was a soap opera Junkie. We all used to be back in the day, but obviously some of us grew out of it! "I need you to do me a favor that no matter what happens, only you and I will know about it. Can you do that for me?" I asked. "Of course homey, whatcha need?" "I need you to go to the Crystal Palace tonight. You remember my boy Brian right?" "From Linden? yeah, of course…what's up?" "Tonight, I need you and him to 'stop by' the Palace. I didn't tell Brian anything about Brianna, he just wants to go out." "What am I suppose to do when I get there? It's not like she doesn't know me!" "Know what T., I really don't care at this point WHAT Brianna thinks. She can't throw you out. It's not like she's the owner!"

"I hear you man, it's just that I like Brianna and I would hate for her to think that I am in there spying on her." "Just don't make it seem that obvious," I said. "Hell, wear a wig and some glasses who cares! Again, I could care less! You are MY boy, not hers!" I said with somewhat of an attitude now. I really didn't want to put T. in this situation, but he was the only one I could trust to hold whatever happened that night between him and I. "Here, take Brian's number. Call him when you are ready. I will be here all night, so call me whenever you get there or whenever you get back or while you're there, or whatever…just call me." "Cool"

Knowing them, they would not be arriving until after midnight and it was only after eight. What was I gonna do until I heard from T? Call Zora! Zora and I were spending time together, but it wasn't like I was trying to GET with her. She was really, truly just a friend. Not that I couldn't see myself being with her, but I was just so into Brianna that I didn't even think that way about other women. Zora was really good to talk to.

(phone rings) "Hello" "Hello Zora, are you in the middle of something?" I asked. "Just finishing up some painting, why what's up?" "I'm calling to see if you wanna come over? I'm not doing anything special. I wanted to see if you could bring some of your CD's for me to copy into my laptop?" "Yeah, I

suppose I can do that. Only if we can go and get some ice cream first. I've got a craving for some Chocolate Mocha nut crunch." "Cool" I said, "but what about all the jogging and all you are doing? Wouldn't buying ice cream be somewhat of a setback?" I asked. "Oh, so you got jokes now Jay...Leno?" Trust me, Zora was tight! I was just teasing her! "I'll be over in a few knuckle head."

I was trying to decide whether or not to tell Zora that I had T. spying on the Crystal Palace tonight, but something told me she would understand.

After she came over, and we were about to leave, I stopped her at the front door.
"Can I tell you something?" I asked. "Go ahead" "I have T. and another friend of mine 'droppin' in' on the Crystal Palace tonight. I really need to see what's going on Zora." "So you tell your FRIEND to go in and see what was up?" she asked as if she couldn't believe I did that. "I can't believe you did that!" (See, I told you) "When I mentioned finding out what was going on there, I meant for YOU to be the one to find out on your own. If it was something bad, why would you want your friends to walk into that number one and number two, why would you embarrass HER like that. If it was you, it would be understandable, but for it to be your boy, doesn't look too good for you Jay. Also, just think if it ISN'T anything negative. Then you will REALLY look like a fool to her." I didn't think of it that way, but she has a point.

"Give me one second." I hurried into to room to call T. and tell him that I've changed my mind, but no one answered his phone when I called. I also called Brian only to get his answering machine as well. It was only after ten, but they must've left already. Now I had to sit here and sweat it out until I heard from T.

Zora and I reached Bruster's. She was really craving that Ice cream. As much as I enjoy spending time with Zora, my mind was only on Brianna this night. I was really hoping and praying that the Lord would not do this to me...not now. "God please don't let this situation turn out bad for Bri and I. I really love this woman and it would really hurt me if something was going on that would prevent us from being together." *How would I feel if T. told me that Brianna was a stripper or something? What would I do? Would I stay with her? If she was a stripper, what kind of strip club was it? Did the dancers get off the stage and give lap dances and things like that? Were they allowed to be groped, touched, kissed...all in the name of T.I.P.S.?(tips)*

I tried to talk to Zora about her work, and what was going on with her, but my mind could not help but think what was going on with Bri. We made our way back to the house, and as I put the key in the door, my phone was ringing. From the caller ID I could see it was a Jersey number, but it was one I didn't recognize. I also missed the call. When I tried to call back, it must've rang 22 times before someone answered. All I heard was music and people in the background.
"Crystal Palace" *the male voice said. I hung up. I don't know if it was Brianna or T. calling me! Now I was REALLY panicking! What if it WAS Brianna calling because she spotted T. and was calling to tell me how sick I was and that she was breaking up with me? Or, maybe it WAS T.! I couldn't ask for either person though, so I just had to wait until whomever it was called back.*

Zora and I copied music to my computer for the next few hours. She had gotten tired and had fallen asleep on the rug on my living room floor. I was still wide awake, with all types of thoughts going thru my mind. It was now after 1am and I was getting hungry. I hadn't eaten all night...worried. I was on my way into the kitchen when the telephone rang. It was T-mac's home number. My first thought was "Ok, now I'm gonna get the truth!" "T-what's up?" "I just got home," *he said.* "Are you sitting down my brother?" *I KNEW IT!! (I said to myself) Although I had suspicions after the airport incident, I didn't want T. to think I could be so gullible, so I was all prepared to act surprised.* "Jay, I'm ya boy, and you know I wouldn't lie to you, but it did not look good playa." "Go ahead man, give it to me like it is T!" *now I was upset.* "The Crystal Palace is a 'Gentlemen's club' Jay." "So what you are saying basically is it's a strip joint?" *I asked.* "Man, it's butt naked women ALL OVER that place!" *T. said.* "They have booths, private booths, private rooms…the whole nine yards man." *Ok, that much I kinda began to feel anyway,* "But what about Brianna?" *I asked.* "Did you see her?" *I asked not really wanting to know the answer.* "Yeah dude, I saw Brianna. I don't know how you are going to handle this, but when we walked in after getting checked by bouncers, the first thing you see is a huge stage with a bar going all the way around it. Then there are tables on the floor and booths along the side of the walls. There were around 6 girls dancing on stage and what seemed like hundreds on the floor, mixing and mingling with the guests. Many giving private dances. Brianna was sitting in a booth with two white guys with suits. At first I couldn't tell it was her, but she got up once and went into a back room and came out and sat down again. Jay, your girl had on the shortest, tightest shorts I have ever seen and a skin tight top that only covered the top part of her chest. Everything else was bare." *My heart sunk! At that moment, I felt like the biggest fool that ever lived. Love? To hell with love! I'm through! Just when I feel I've met…excuse me, God SENDS me someone that I can finally let go with and actually WANT to give my heart to, she is a stripper! Isn't that just my luck!* "Did she see you?" *I asked.* "Naw man not at all. After I saw her, I got sick to my stomach and told Brian that I didn't feel like stayin'. Since we both drove, I told him I was out. He stayed. Yo man, I know you feel like crap right now, but maybe it was best that you found this out before you went and married her. You do know that everything happens for a reason my brother." "Yeah man, I know. I appreciate your help T. and whatever you do, please, keep this between you and I. Definitely do not tell that fool Darryl. He'll clown me for the next 10 years about this!" "No problem Jay. Sorry man. Call me if you need me." "I will, talk to you soon."

I sat there on the side of the bed for what seemed like hours holding my head in my hands. So much ran through my mind. Just picturing my woman sharing herself with all these different guys was driving me crazy! Zora was still in the living room asleep, but it was getting late so I had to wake her up. She had church the next morning. "Zora, it's pretty late hon. Let me walk you home." "Ok" she said. On the way I told her what had been revealed to me...that Brianna was a stripper. "So, what are you gonna do now?" she asked still half asleep. "I have no idea Zora. I guess I really need to rethink this relationship. If she has been keeping this from me, who knows what other skeletons she has in her closet. I feel like the biggest fool! Here I am out here, making a life for US, not ME...US and she is there flirting with guys and giving them private lap dances!? I really can't do this. The trust is definitely gone and without trust, there is no relationship." "Maybe you need to speak with her before you make any hasty decisions Jay. Maybe there is a reason she hasn't told you. You never know. I'm only giving her the benefit of the doubt because I am a woman as well, and if it was me, I would want my man to hear me out." "So you would keep something like that from your man too?" I asked. "When you first came over my house, and saw my pictures and asked what I did for a living, was there any hesitation in my voice or did I just come out and tell you that I was a nude art instructor?" "Ok, then.... I don't think you need to ask me that question!"

As she opened her door, she turned around and gave me a hug. "Don't worry sweetie, maybe there's a logical explanation. If you need to talk you can call me. I'll be up for a while getting ready for church tomorrow." She said. "Ok, thanks Zora, thank you for being someone I can talk to. You really are a big help to me." As I walked back home, my eyes filled up with tears. Why Brianna? Why did you have to come into MY life?

Damn...a stripper!

Chapter 16

▼

Love don't live here anymore

In retrospect I look back. I guess it was bound to happen. All the hearts I have broken in the past, it is only the law of averages that would dictate that eventually my day would come. Well it's here, and it does not feel good! I guess everything happens for a reason, although I had no idea what was on God's mind with this one. It is also a good thing that this job opportunity came up because if I would have had to be around Brianna, it would have driven me crazy. Not to say that it will be easy to forget her, but it would have been much harder if I was able to be around her.

Now, when should I tell her that I know what her role in the 'entertainment industry' really consist of? I was not going to call her immediately, although I wanted to. Maybe I would just wait until she calls me. I knew she would be calling me tomorrow (Sunday). Besides, I needed time to think about what I was going to say to her.

Sunday morning came, and as expected, my phone rang around 8:30. I didn't even have to check the caller ID. I knew it was her. "Good morning baby, how are you?" she asked. "Sleepy!" I said in a hostile tone. "Why, what did YOU do last night that has you so tired this morning?" Funny, but the voice that used to bring me so much calm and peace now seemed to rile me. "I stayed up most of the night thinking of what I was going to say to you this morning when you called." "What do you mean? Is there something you need to say to me?" she asked. "There's a WHOLE LOT I have to say to you Brianna, but first let me ask you... how long did you think it would be before I found out the truth about you? How long did you expect to keep lying to me?!" "Ok, you are scaring me now baby, what's wrong?" "Your man in the airport... did you give him a lap dance he'll never forget? Is that what happened? "Jay..." "I don't want to hear it Brianna! You lied to me! You are a stripper at the Crystal Palace and you felt that is something you had to keep from me?! What happened to the love you said you had for me Brianna? You've been misleading me the whole time. All those nights I tried to be understanding about your job and how you were an entertainment manager, and all that garbage you used to run by me! I believed you. I believed IN you! I introduced you to my mom, my children, my friends...and all you've been doing is lying to me?!" All I could hear was her bawling. She was crying like a baby. "Jay baby, please listen...." "No! I don't wanna listen to you anymore! I am through listening to you! For what, so you can tell me more lies?!" "Jay I am sorry baby! Please listen to me for a second..." "I can't Brianna. God knew what he was doing getting me away from you. I didn't understand why at first but now I do. Is THAT why you couldn't move here with me now? Your CLIENTS wouldn't understand? All this time I was thinking I was first in your life only to find out that I am not even on the radar?! You chose to stay at a STRIP CLUB, instead of coming with me?! And we went to church together!!!! Every Sunday?! How can you LIVE with yourself Brianna?!" Again, she broke down crying.

"I am hanging up now. Please do me a favor and don't ever call my number again!" I said. "Game time is over. Tell all of your well paying customers that your ex-fiancee...yes EX! said that they are a bunch of really lucky guys. They saw more of you than I did!" "So it's over Jay, just like that?" she *said trying to catch her breath from crying so hard. "It's over Brianna. I wish you a happy, successful life and may you get all that you deserve." I said sarcastically. "Before you go Jay, there is something you need to know." "I don't need to know anything. I know all I need to know. Have a nice life," and I hung up.*

She must've called my phone ninety times the rest of the morning. Obviously, she didn't go to church. I did not want to take her calls. I wouldn't take ANY more of her calls. That was it for me. Love didn't live here anymore! I need to go back to the way I used to be. Who needs to settle down? The truth is, it felt really, really good being in love. Having those feelings for the first time in my life was a blessing, because now at least I know how it feels. I'm not going to sit here and say that I will NEVER fall in love again, but definitely not anytime soon. Besides I had a new position to keep me occupied and I had a new friend in Zora, who I know would be more than happy to get to know me better as well. It wasn't like I really wanted to get with her or anything, but she was real easy to talk to and fun to hang out with. I really wanted to keep her more as my friend. Besides, Charlotte had LOTS of available young African American sisters that would love to meet a single, handsome, well paid executive, but I knew I would miss Brianna. We had built so much together and had so many plans for the future. All of that went up in a cloud of smoke. Gone. She took my entire future away from me by lying to me. In actuality, she killed a very big part of my heart.

All that day I did nothing but lay around. Zora called me a few times in between Brianna's calls. We spoke, but not about anything major. She was pretty upset that I didn't even give Brianna a chance to explain. I don't know if it was HER who wanted to know, or because she was a woman and if it was her, she would want me to give her the chance to explain as well. You know, a woman sticking up for another woman. I really didn't feel like any company or doing anything that day, so I told her I would hook up with her early in the week. The only one I did call was T. and told him what happened. He totally understood and just told me to take it easy and not rush into any new relationships out of anger. He was well aware of Zora and warned me to steer clear or else I might end up hurting her just as I had been hurt. He was right, and I totally understood. I wasn't trying to hurt anyone else, but I still wasn't trying to settle down anymore for a while either.

The next few days, work was a priority. Brianna did keep trying to reach me, however. She was sending email after email. A few I started to read....

"Jay, I understand that you no longer wish to talk to me. I miss you so much it hurts. I still can't get over the fact that I hurt you as much as I did. I really wish you would just listen to me for a minute. I have something very important to tell you, something that I think you should know...."

I would delete it at that point. What more could she tell me? Maybe she was gay as well. That's why all the pictures of women in her house. Nothing would surprise me at this point, but I just didn't want to hear it. It was time to get Brianna off my mind and start to get back into Jay.

I happened to hear that on Wednesdays after work, they had a nice little Jazz club that only certain types of individuals attended. I had decided early on that day at work that I would stop by and check the spot out. True to the word, it was a really nice spot! Quiet, dark, jazz band playin and full of beautiful women.
I had a seat at the bar and ordered a coke. I was really feelin' the music and trying my best to get Brianna off my mind, but I thought.... I wondered what she was doing at that very moment. I took a sip of coke from my glass and glanced to my right. I happen to notice a familiar face, sitting at a table for two, dim light and all. It was Zora, sitting with some brother in a suit. They were sitting across from each other, but they still looked as if they were enjoying each others conversation.

I really wanted to say something but before I could, she noticed me and asked me to come over. I really wasn't in the mood, but I went anyway. "Hey Jay, what are YOU doing here?" "What's up Zora!" trying to act like I was Ok with her sitting there with another guy. "Brian this is my neighbor and friend Jay, Jay this is my co-worker Brian." We shook hands and exchanged pleasantries…FAKE pleasantries. The whole time I was checkin dude trying to figure out what HE thought it (him and Zora) was. "Listen, I'm not going to stay. You two can get back into whatever…well, you know." I think Zora thought I was a little upset and asked if she could talk to me for a minute. "Yeah, yeah what's up Z.?" looking confused. We stepped away from her table and walked towards the front of the club. "Listen, I really want you to know that there's nothing going on between Brian and I. He is strictly a co-worker and asked if I would be interested in sharing a drink with him. He's actually married." "Zora you don't owe me an explanation luv!" "You and I are just friends. You respect me that way and I respect you the same. I would never interfere with whatever you have going on personally with whomever you have it going on with." "I understand that Jay and I appreciate it, but I will leave with you right now if you think it will be a problem between us!" Needless to say, I'm standing there now with my mouth wide open. I can't believe she just came out like that! "Is there something we need to talk about Zora?" I asked. "We can talk about whatever you wanna talk about, whenever you wanna talk about it!" DAMN! I really didn't think I had that type of effect on Zora. Put it this way, she has never really come out and shown it. "I've been here for an hour and a half with Brian and the whole time, I've been thinking about you," She said. "Forgive me for being so blunt and honest, but I don't want you to get it confused because you saw me out with another man. Not that I don't respect your woman nor do I hope you think that I am not sympathetic to the problems you are having, but I would have to be crazy not to see that a man like you is different…different in a good way." She gave me this really cute smile. At that point, I really didn't know what to say. "Listen, you go back over there to your date and we'll talk about it tomorrow." "I keep telling you he's not a date!" "Ok, Ok…we'll talk tomorrow." I grab the end of her chin and tilted her head upward…then I bent down and kissed her! She looked as surprised as I was! I really had no set plan to do that. It was just a reaction. If you thought we were confused, you should've seen the look on Brian's face!

I walked away and went home. Not really knowing what to think, about anything. I was tired of thinking. Tired of feeling. I really wanted to just not care. Now I understand why it is I've always held on to my heart. In fear of something exactly like this happening. As much as women say it's so hard to find a good man, It's just as hard for a man to find a good woman.

A lot of men today feel as though the new millennium women are a lot harder to deal with than women, say from my mom's era. There was different sense of loyalty, sense of commitment. Women then had a certain pride about the way they did ANYTHING! The way they carried themselves, even though they didn't get the respect they deserved. Even though they had a man who wasn't worth the draws he put on in the morning, they stuck with that man and did what they had to do in every other area, especially the areas that the man fell short. She was a woman. It didn't have to be anything about any other man. Even flirting was forbidden. I know it may sound like a double standard because men have been doing it for a long time, but women generally hold themselves to a higher standard…or so it USED to be. You always find a woman up in a man's face nowadays, then always try to blame it on a man. I know it's a fact because of the amount of married and so-called committed women that approach me regularly. I'm sure their men have no idea what THEY are up to!"

About an hour and a half after I arrived home, Zora was at my door. "Hey Zora, what's up luv?" "I hope you don't mind me just dropping in, but I needed to know what that kiss at the club was REALLY about and I decided to find that out in person." I stepped back and let her in. She took off her coat and hung it up in my hall closet. She picked up her bag and made her way to the living room. I followed her. She went and stood in front of my T.V. and opened her bag. She reached inside and pulled out a canvas, a few jars of paint, a few paintbrushes, and a small easel. First she unbuttoned her blouse. Then she reached around back and zipped down her skirt and slid it off. She unbuttoned her bra and slid it off. Lastly she turned around and slid off her bikinis. She slowly turned back around and handed me the paint and brush. "Paint me!"

(phone rings) (looking around on the bed for the phone—after 10 seconds or so I answered) "Hello?" "Jay, what is going on, what's all that noise?" It was Zora. "I was on my way to work and I just wanted to see if we can get together later on. We really need to talk about that kiss. Don't think I forgot!" "O…o…o…K?!" Man, I must've fallen asleep as soon as I got in last night!

Wow! Now THAT was a dream!

Chapter 17

The Phone call

Almost a month had passed and the holidays were approaching quickly. I still hadn't spoken to Brianna. I did begin to save her emails however. By this point, she was down to maybe five a week. My lack of response had begun to break her down. I'm sensing that she's giving up and realizing that she and I are over with. Maybe one day, when I was really over her, I would look back on her emails and be able to read them without wanting to put my fist through my computer screen.

Work was keeping me extremely busy and Zora and I spent time together whenever I had the spare time. Darryl had called me a few days earlier and told me he wanted to come down the coming weekend. He said he wanted to come and check me out for a few days, but I know Denise really held the Ace of spades in that matter. It was cool, I understood. I myself had plans to go back home in the next two weeks anyway. I did not want to spend Thanksgiving and Christmas in Charlotte. Charlotte was good to me in a lot of ways, but some things could never replace home. I called Zora to let her know that Darryl was coming down for the weekend. "Is he really!" She said happily. "Good, now all four of us can hang out this weekend. What day is he coming, Friday or Saturday?" she asked. "I don't know, he didn't say. Why do you ask?" "Saturday, I have an afternoon class and guess who is gonna be the model. I was going to invite him and Denise!"

Zora loved show off her body, but I couldn't let that happen, not with my boy. "Naw, we'll pass," I said. "What's wrong Jay, don't want your boy getting a look at this huh?" I could imagine her turning around to showoff her beautifully sculptured, hand crafted, grade-A behind! "Whatever! Darryl won't be witnessing you getting painted in the nude that's for Damn sure! Besides, I have a few things to do at the church Saturday, and if he's here, I'm sure he is going to be with Denise. I KNOW he won't be looking to roll with me."

I had found another Church home. It was really, a really powerful sanctuary. You could feel the Holy Ghost as soon as you entered the door.... (If you were saved that is) The Pastor was around my age, and he was very honest in his delivery of the word. He would tell you just how it was good or bad, like it or not. His favorite saying was, "if you don't like what I'm about to say...exit, exit, exit, and exit." He would point one by one to each exit. It was that honesty that led me to fall in love with Spiritual Mercies Christian Church. In a little over a month, I had made myself known in the church, and not just for making large tithes. I had joined the prison ministry, and the drug and alcohol ministry in hopes of helping some of my brothers and sisters that were out there still struggling, or those locked up and seeking God in their lives. Fortunately, it's never too late for Jesus. It was a beautiful thing and I enjoyed doing whatever I can. It also helped to have other things going on in my life besides working and thinking about Brianna. Of course I still loved her. I really wish she had been honest with me. I don't know how I would have handled it, but it would have been better than just finding out the way I did. See, I never understood how a woman could tell me to "just tell the truth. It would be so much easier for me if I knew." "HOW?" would be my answer to myself. I can't do that, so I will keep the lie going in hopes you will never find out in hopes that I don't end up hurting you. Now I know how it feels to be on the other end. I was praying daily that God would place in me the heart to forgive Brianna. I wanted to call her and tell her I forgive her. I wasn't ready for us to get back together or go on with the wedding plans or anything like that. I just wanted her to know that I forgave her. I really just wanted to hear her voice. I missed her so much. As much as I like Zora, she could never be Brianna.

What I decided was that there was one of two things I could do. Totally forget Brianna Williams ever existed, or call her, LISTEN to her and see what comes out of it. I decided to make the phone call. Tomorrow…Friday night, I would call her. I would probably get her answering machine because I know on a Friday night she would be at that…at work. Her answering machine would probably have been better anyway. This way I could leave a message for her to call me. That should really make her happy!

The next day at work, all I could think about was what I was going to say to her. Should I tell her how much I miss her? Should I be angry and forget all about trying to be nice? What would God want me to say to her?

Finally, the work day was over. The first thing I did when I got home was call Zora to tell her what my plans were. "I think I'm ready to hear what Brianna has to say now," I told her. "Well, it's about time. You know this is the only way you are really going to see where you two stand. If it's not going to be (you and her) you will know after you speak to her. If it is, you will know that as well."
"When are you going to call her?" she asked. "A little later on I guess." "Well, you make sure you call me afterwards. I wanna hear all about it!" "You know you're my girl Zora! I really want to thank you again for being here for me as much as you have since you met me. You are a true friend and I will always love you for that. No matter what happens between Brianna and I." "Awwww, I love you too Jay. I just want to see you happy. If you're not going to be with me, it may as well be Brianna!" We started laughing.

Next thing I needed to do was call Darryl and see when he was leaving, tonight or tomorrow. I called his house but no one answered. That was unusual. He is ALWAYS home at this time. Unless, he is on his way here, but I don't know why he would just come without telling me what time he was arriving. Maybe he called Denise and asked HER to pick him up. After a call to Zora to find out if she'd heard from Denise, I know he wasn't on his way tonight. Denise and Zora were going out and Denise had not heard from Darryl. Where the heck can he be? I decided to lay down and take a nap before I called Brianna. I will tell you this—it was the most uncomfortable nap I had taken in recent memory. I just kept tossing and turning, and I couldn't figure out why. I just had an uneasy feeling. Maybe I was anxious about calling Brianna. Yeah, that was it! After tossing and turning for another hour or so, I decided to call. It wasn't as late as I wanted to be initially, I might even still catch her home, but I wanted to get it over with. I went into the bathroom and washed my face. Then I went to the kitchen and got a glass of water, went back to my bedroom and sat on the side of my bed, next to the phone. Before I picked up the phone, I got down on my knees and prayed for God to give me the right words to say to this woman. To take all of the anger and bitterness out of my heart, even if it's just for a moment and allow me to talk with reason. Whatever happened after that I would leave in his hands.

I picked up the phone to call but before it could even get to the first ring, my other line beeped. I saw that it was Darryl, and I needed to talk to him so I clicked over quickly to tell him to hold on, "D-hold on for one second man, I'm on the other line," I said in a hurried tone. "Jay, hold on man...don't put me on hold...wait a minute!" I clicked back over. "Hello, who is this?.... Hello, hello...who is this?" a voice said. "This is Jay, who is this?" I asked. I could tell something was wrong. "Jay this is Karen...something has happened Jay," she was crying...crying hysterically! "Karen, what is it? Where's Brianna?" "Jay..." someone else took the phone. "Jay this is Mrs. Williams baby. I have something really terrible to tell you. The police just left here. They found Brianna's body this morning. She was raped and murdered and left by the side of the road. Her body was found about a mile from the Crystal Palace..." there was silence. I could hear people in the background sobbing, and screaming! I dropped the phone and stood up. No, this can't be true! There must be a mistake. Brianna would not have allowed herself to be killed. I picked up the phone and asked Mrs. Williams to hold on one second. I clicked back over to Darryl. All I could hear was him sobbing. *"Darryl are you there?" "Jay man, Brianna was killed. It's all over the news. Karen just called and told me about ten minutes ago. I rushed over here as soon as she told me." "Jay, are you there?" Jay..."* All I could do was sit there with the phone in my hand. I could not believe Brianna was gone. MURDERED! RAPED! She didn't just die, she suffered! And I wasn't there for her! I broke down and cried like a baby for at least 30 minutes. My heart, the soul of my soul was gone! Now I know that's why I couldn't rest...my soul knew something was wrong. I had to get to Jersey.

As I stood up and dried my face, the phone rang again. It was my mom. I couldn't take the call. I knew she would be worried sick about me, but I could not talk to her right then. She would have been asking me question after question and I was in no position to answer them. I had to get to Brianna! Maybe she didn't die. Maybe she is in the hospital just beat up bad and she will wake up. I need to be there! Right now I was in denial. I called up Zora and asked her to take me the airport. I didn't tell her what had happened until we were on our way. She saw my eyes red and my face swollen from crying and she knew it was bad...she just didn't know HOW bad, until I told her. She almost ran off the road when I did. I had to hurry and get to the airport. Last flight was at 9:40 and that was about 45 minutes away. God was definitely with me because we made it with time for me to buy a last minute ticket and still had to wait about 15 minutes before we boarded.

I couldn't believe Brianna was gone. I must have cried the whole trip back to Jersey. I kept seeing her face trying to explain to me and me pushing her away. Even though it never happened quite that way that is the vision I kept seeing. The flight attendant kept asking me if I was Ok, but once I told her I had lost someone very close to me, that I had lost my fiancée, she understood and left me alone for the rest of the flight.

When I arrived in Jersey an hour and forty five minutes later, I flagged a taxi and went straight to Brianna's house. I asked the driver to get me there as quickly as possible and gave him a $100 dollar bill, I was there in 11 minutes—(it would have normally taken me about 30 min.)

When we turned on the street, all we could see were cars. He couldn't even get CLOSE to the house. I jumped out the taxi and ran to the house. There were so many people in Brianna's house. Her mom, family, friend, detectives had just pulled up…my head was spinning. I managed to find my way to her mom and she saw me and turned around and grabbed me. "Jay, my baby is gone." She wasn't crying, but I could tell she had been. "That rat bastard killed her Jay. He raped her and he killed her." About that time, Karen walked over still crying hysterically. I grabbed her and held her tight. Darryl came over to us as well. "What happened?" I asked. Karen started to tell me but broke down again and walked away. "Why did you leave her Jay?" her mother asked. "Brianna loved you more than she has ever loved any man, ever. Believe me I know. She would talk to me and tell me all that she felt for you. You were special to her Jay, very special and when you left like you did it killed her. All she wanted was for you to trust her." "Mrs. Williams Brianna was my life. Everything I've done was for her. Me moving away to start a better life was for HER! I could've stayed here in Jersey and been Ok if it was just me. Everything I did, I did for her! Then I find out she lied to me the whole time about what type of work she did. Why couldn't she be honest with ME?!" Now I was crying again. "She hurt me Mrs. Williams, she hurt me…but I was calling to forgive her. To tell her I loved her and that I needed for us to be one again. I couldn't do it! No matter how much I tried, I couldn't forget about her.

That's why I was calling Mrs. Williams, to tell Brianna I was sorry for not hearing her out and that I forgave her for keeping such a terrible secret from me. We were meant to be together. God would have softened my heart, but I needed her!" Mrs. Williams put her arms around me and sat me down. I felt like I was about to pass out. "Jay, Brianna told me why you and she weren't speaking. You are right, she wasn't honest with you. She lied. She lied because she was embarrassed and it is her father to blame for that." Now, I'm really confused. "Her father?" "What does THAT mean?" "Jay, Brianna told me you thought she was a stripper and that every time she tried to explain to you, you wouldn't hear what she had to say, but if you weren't so stubborn, you would have heard her say that she was not a stripper at the Palace, she owned the Palace! Her father left it to her when he passed. It was HIS club. He always felt that only a woman could run a gentlemen's club the way it should've been run and since Brianna was the love of his life, it only made sense to him to will it to her and when she was old enough she would take over once he passed. Brianna HATED it, but she didn't want to let her father down. She stuggled with this daily. She was a Christian woman trying her best to live in God's word, but she was left with the burden of carrying on her fathers wishes. Her father was the closest person to her, and she really didn't want to let him down, even after he was gone. So she kept up that club despite her beliefs, for her father's sake. The good news is that since you came along, and then proposed this move to her, she was ready to get out. She was in the process of selling it, just so she can come to be with you. She had been meeting with the same two guys for the past month or so and I believe they had just completed the deal (the two white guys T. saw her with at the club that night), now this!"

How stupid do I feel! All this time, she WASN'T a stripper, but owned the club! It was told to me later on that night that she used to dress the part but never participated in any type of non-descript action…with ANYONE! All the girls in the pictures all over her house were girls that either used to or still did dance at the Palace. Some even when her father was still owner. That's why she couldn't just up and leave and come with me, she had to sell the club first. "Why didn't she trust me enough to tell me all this Mrs. Williams?" *I asked.* "She didn't want to lose you. She feared that you being a Christian man and all, would cut her loose if you found out she owned such a place." "She never had a problem telling anyone else she was with, but she just couldn't with you."

After sitting there until the next morning, Darryl and I left and went to my mothers house. She'd already heard and had been up all night crying about Brianna and worried about me. "I'm fine mom. I just need to get some sleep. Brianna's mom and I are going over to the morgue in a little while to identify her." *I went into the bathroom, ran some water and just cried. I cried myself to sleep right there on the bathroom floor.*

After a while I heard my mom banging on the door. "Are you Ok in there Jay?" "Yeah mom, I'm fine. I'll be out in a minute" *I came out the bathroom and laid on the sofa. My mom tried to feed me, but I didn't have an appetite. I called Mrs. Williams and told her I would be there in a few hours, then I called Darryl and asked if he could take me. He told me that Curt and T-mac were looking for me as well.*

I can't believe Brianna is gone. My life…my future wife is gone. It would only take a short time before the projects in me showed its ugly face. Finding out who did this and seeking revenge weren't far behind. I know I am a child of God now, but I've got questions for God. I don't understand him at all right now.

Chapter 18

Questioning God

The next day was filled with much despair. I was not going in to view the body with Mrs. Williams, I would not be able to take seeing Brianna any way other than I know her to look. To this day, I have never been to a viewing and I have never been to a funeral. Those types of events would leave too lasting of a memory for me, so I would always stay behind at whomever's house was going to be the spot after the funeral. I took the ride with Mrs. Williams because I know Brianna wouldn't have wanted her mother going there alone.

The ride there was brutal. I was filled with so much grief, only God was able to hold me and keep me upright. I felt like dying too. I thought so much of Brianna. Her smile, her silliness, her tender love and affection, her kindness to others, and most of all, her love for me. When I left for Charlotte, I know that had to be the hardest thing for her to deal with, and I didn't consider once how she felt. Regardless, I knew she had my back. I knew she would ALWAYS have my back. Yet I was not there for her. In the time she needed me the most, when her life was in danger, I failed her!

How could I have not been there for her? God why, why did you move me so far away from Brianna? Why did you allow the devil to stick his ugly face in our relationship and cause the friction that he caused? Hadn't we proven to you that we were united in YOUR name together, as one? We served you, we worshiped you and we begged your forgiveness when pleasures of the flesh took over and out ruled our loyalty to you and your word.

(I began to talk out loud) "You said at if we wanted forgiveness all we had to do was ask!" I ASKED GOD! I ASKED…WE ASKED! AND YOU TURNED YOUR BACK ON US? YOU ALLOW SOMETHING LIKE THIS TO HAPPEN TO BRIANNA? WHERE WERE YOU GOD? WHEN I LEFT AND PRAYED TO YOU TO TAKE CARE OF BRIANNA, YOU TOLD ME TO GO AHEAD…THAT IT WOULD BE ALRIGHT!! THIS IS NOT ALRIGHT GOD! THIS IS WRONG! THIS IS REALLY, REALLY WRONG! WHAT AM I GONNA DO NOW?!?!?" "Jay, calm down baby!" "It's not God's fault. He was ready for his baby to come home, that's all." Mrs. Williams had a calming voice. A voice of experience. "Don't you ever go blaming God for the brutal act some deranged man performed. That man should be responsible for his own actions. God had nothing to do with that. All that was taken was the flesh Jay, Brianna's spirit will live forever." She was right, but I still wasn't trying to hear it. I was hurt. Devastated. I had never lost a close, real close, loved one before, so I had no idea how to react.

Even though I blamed God, I still prayed to him.

We arrived at the coroners shortly after. Darryl and Mrs. Williams went in. I couldn't do it, so I stayed in the car. I was really hoping they would come out and say that it wasn't her, but the police said she had all of her ID on her. Fifteen minutes later, they came out. Darryl was holding Mrs. Williams. I rushed out the car to help out. "Jay, he killed my baby." I looked at Darryl and he was wiping the tears from his eyes. We helped her back to the car and Darryl drove us back to Mrs. Williams house. All the way home, she was rockin back and forth hummin'. "The man said that they are about to take her to have an autopsy done. A detective will be by later on," she said.

I decided to go back to Mrs. Williams house with her so that I could be there when the detective came. By the time we got there, the house was packed with people. I didn't feel like sitting in the living room, so I asked Mrs. Williams if I could use the computer she had in one of the bedrooms. I wanted to check Brianna's emails to me. The one's I saved. She said it would be fine and told me that I could go in her bedroom. She had a laptop there and a internet connection, so it was easy for me to log into my email account. It really felt kinda funny to open these emails and read them now, after Brianna is gone. I know it's going to feel like she is speaking to me.

From: Brianna
Sent: 11/04/85
Subject: Please read this email!

Jay, I don't know why you would not take my phone calls. I want to speak to you to explain. You have it all wrong! When I told you I love you, I meant it. I would never do anything to hurt you Jay. It is really important that you take my calls. You know I really hate talking thru email. Please call me or at least take my call when I call you. I will call you in the morning.

I love you!

Bri

From: Brianna
Sent: 11/05/85
Subject: Please listen....

Jay, baby I called you this morning like I said I would, and you still didn't answer your phone. I am not going to get into anything thru email other than to say that I love you and miss you so much baby!! Maybe one day you will have the nerve to call me and hopefully we can talk. I will tell you again, it's not what you think.

Anyways, I have an attachment to this message that I really want you to listen to.

I love you Jay!

Bri

I clicked on the attachement...a song began to play. It was like Brianna was sitting right beside me, talking to me....

(Xscape-The arms of the one who love's you)

> I know you're going, I can't make you stay
> I can only let you know I'll love you anyways
> And if the road you take, leads to heartbreak
> Somewhere down the line
> If someone ever hurts you, or treats your heart unkind
>
> You just run, to the arms of the one who loves you
> You just run to these arms
> And these two arms will keep you warm
> When rain has filled your heart, never fear
> I'm never far, you just run
> To the arms of the one who loves you
>
> I want you happy, I want the best for you
> And if you have to leave to find your dream,
> I hope that dream comes true
> But if the world you find brings you hard times

Or someone makes you cry
I'll be there to hold you, I'll be standing by

You just run, to the arms of the one who loves you
You'll never have to worry....
You just run to these arms
And these two arms will keep you warm
When rain has filled your heart, never fear
I'm never far, you just run
To the arms of the one who loves you

My love is strong enough you know,
strong enough to let you go,
but I'll always hold you, inside my heart
And if you should have a change in mind
You can come back anytime
And when you do (when you do)
You (you can run...)

It took me a minute after that one to compose myself. Maybe I really didn't know how much Brianna loved me.

From: Brianna

Sent: 11/06/85

Subject: I really need to talk to you!!

Jay, baby I really need to talk to you. I don't know what's going on, but I have not been feeling well lately. Besides, that guy that we saw at the airport that day has been coming around here a lot more since the airport incident. He is starting to scare me. I had to have him escorted out last night. He kept saying all these things he wanted to do to me, and that you have no idea what you have...stuff like that. He used to be nice, but all of a sudden he's becoming aggressive. I am going to make a doctors appointment tomorrow. I don't understand what's wrong with me. I am not sick or anything, but I feel very light headed a lot. I don't know if I'm just physically tired, or tired of thinking and praying for you. Like the song I sent you said. I want you happy Jay. I just want the best for you and if you feel as though I'm not the one, then I have to realize that and let you go on. Maybe one day I will get it. Then again, maybe I never will.

I don't know if you are reading my emails or not, but I hope you are at least doing that since you don't want to speak to me.

I'm so in love with you!

Bri

From: Brianna

Sent 11/07/85

Subject: Doctor's visit

Good morning baby! Well, I went to the doctor's office yesterday. Like I thought, it was nothing major. He gave me some really good vitamins and some iron pills to take. I didn't go to work last night, but someone kept calling my house and hanging up. It was really scary. At first I thought it was you playing around on the phone. I was HOPING it was you anyway, but after doing it for 4 or 5 times, it stopped. I took my pills and rested the rest of the night. I've missed you soooooooo much. I wish you would've been there with me the whole night. I used to feel so safe in your arms Jay. You were my protector. My King, and no matter how many times it happened, I ALWAYS felt honored to be in your arms. You'll always be my King!

I love you,

Bri

I just kept reading, email after email. Crying on most, laughing at some. "Oh wow, here's a few it looks like I missed."

From: Brianna

Sent: 11/15/85 (2 days before her murder)

Subject: Jay, Please call me! I need your help!!

Jay baby, why aren't you calling me. I am sitting here crying my eyes out. So much is going on and you're not around! If you can just TELL me what to do, I will do it, but I need to get out of here Jay. I can't stay here anymore. This guy is really freakin me out. I have filed a restraining order against him, he is banned from the club, yet he manages to find me! I can be out somewhere during the day, and he will just appear. By the time I call the police, he's gone. He keeps saying he wants me and he's gonna get me. I am on the verge of hiring one of the bouncers at the bar to watch my back ALL day and night. Also, I have been really, really sick Jay. Mostly in the morning. It gets better as the day goes on. As for this guy...you know me, I have never been afraid to handle an admirer, but this guy is different. You see how big he is! He has gotten to me and I just really need to get out of here. Please call me and let's talk.

I am in love with you!

Bri

From: Brianna

Sent: 11/16/85

Subject: I'm scared baby!

Jay, honey, I have to leave here! This guy is after me! He knows where I live and everything. Rocco (the bouncer) has a few things to do during the day, so he's not available all day. There's about 4-5 hours when he can't be with me. I am terrified. I am not going to work or anything although I do have to go by there tomorrow. I have a very important meeting. No, it's not what you think. I am going to explain to you very soon baby, but right now I need you to call me and get me out of here. If I knew your address, I would just come on my own. I can't even remember your friends' numbers. But Karen told me to call Darryl and Darryl would talk to you. She is getting me his number. I am also very sick baby. I definitely have to see a doctor again, but I'd rather wait until I get there with you. So that you can take care of me! I will be in touch VERY soon whether you like it or not. Don't pick up the phone!...I will be there shortly anyway punk!!

P.s. I have something very exciting to tell you!!

See you soon, I love you!

Bri

That was the last email I had gotten from her. Right now I am getting a visual of this guy in my head again. I need to be able to describe him to the police if they don't already know what he looks like. She was on her way to me! Wow! If she would have rang my doorbell, I know I would have forgotten all about being mad.

Later on that day, I was still at Brianna's mom's house. The lead detective and his partner on the case came over to update us on what was going on. First thing they said was that it would take a few days to determine the exact cause of death, but said she was raped, beaten and strangled. They believe she died from asphyxiation, but couldn't rule out blunt trauma to the head. She had deep bruises on her head as well as hand marks around her neck. They are talking to people and have a few suspects in mind, one in particular. They mentioned the dude from the bar, but brushed it off as it was no big deal. I didn't tell them about the emails yet. I want to see if this guy turns out to be the main suspect. I have my own plans for him.

The detective told us one more thing...another blow was dealt. Brianna was pregnant! She was about 5 weeks they believe, and it may have been the trauma from the rape that killed the baby. Again, when the autopsy was complete we would know more. That's what she wanted to tell me when she got to me. That she was carrying our child! Now the person who killed her would be charged with both murders whenever he is found! He better hope he's found by the police before I find him! That type of justice needs no judge or jury. After hearing about Brianna's pregnancy, Mrs. Williams lost it...completely. Our baby would have been her first grandchild. Everyone in the house began crying again, it was another day of sadness.

Chapter 19

▼

Painful Lessons

After making it through the day, I called Darryl to pick me up. I wanted to stay with him for the night. I called my mom and explained everything to her. She was totally devastated, especially when I told her she almost had another grandchild. She cried, and she cried. My mom is extremely spiritual and like Mrs. Williams, she too felt Brianna was in a better place. I just was not able to wrap my mind around that quite yet. I was no longer blaming God, but I had other things on my mind at that time. "Don't you go and do anything stupid," was the last thing she said to me before we hung up. "Don't worry about me mom, I'll be fine."

"So what are you gonna do now?" Darryl asked. "First thing I am gonna do is find out if there are any more clubs in the area like the Palace," I said. "Why?" he asked. "Brianna sent me a few emails D. and told me that the guy that we saw at the airport that morning when Brianna and I were on our way to Charlotte, was harassing her. She was terrified of him and even had a restraining order out on him. The last email she sent me said he knew where she lived and everything. This guy is the one who killed her Darryl, and I am going to hunt him down and treat him like the animal that he is. He deserves that!" "If she had a restraining order out on him, then he HAS to be a prime suspect wouldn't you think? Did the detectives mention him?" "Yeah, they described him, but they don't have a clue." "Did you tell them about the emails?" "Not yet, I don't want them to know about any of that just yet."

"That might cause them to find him and pick him up for questioning and all and it would make it real tough to get to him then because I am sure they will be watching him." "Oh, I see, so your plan is to handle this yourself then end up in jail huh? That's your plan?" "D—he killed my wife! He killed my unborn child! He's taken everything away from me! What difference does it make now what happens to me?" "You have two other children and a lot of family and friends that would be crushed if something happens to you. Come on man, you're the Christian here. Aren't you supposed to let God handle situations like this?" "I understand what you're saying my brother, but some things a man just gotta do!"

I got the phone book out and began searching the area for other 'Gentlemen clubs'. I found two. One was called 'The Chateau' and the other, a club called 'Ordinary Places'. Both were within 25 miles of The Palace, and since this guy likes to frequent clubs and since the Palace is shut down, I'm willing to bet he will visit one of these two, if he hasn't already begun doing so.

The next day I went to Elizabeth. I had Darryl's car. He had an important meeting at work that day, or else he would've stayed home. I dropped him off in the morning and headed downtown Elizabeth. I needed to see a few people I hadn't had a reason to see in the past few years. With Brianna on my mind, and the brutal way she was killed, I had my game face on! I saw a familiar face on First street standing near the Recreation Center. "Yo Cecil, I need to talk to you for a minute!" I yelled out. At first he didn't know who I was and refused to come to the car. I actually had to park and get out before he recognized me. "Jay, my man! Where ya been boy?" he said, like he was happy to see me. "Not down here, that's for sure! Listen, I *need to get my hands on some steel. A 38 (cal) or a 9mm will do just fine. Who can I see?" "What's up Jay? You ok? Need me to round up a few of the fellas?" "Naw man I got this." "See Lil Raymond" he said. Lil Raymond was the son of a friend of mine growing up. I was there when Lil Raymond was born. Now he's the biggest gun runner in the state. "Where can I find him?" I asked. "Most likely on Third street next to the pool hall. He has a room back there." "Cool. Good seeing you again man." I said, and was off to find Lil Ray.*

As promised, he was there. He was on the table (pool) when I walked in. "Jaaaaayyyyy! What the hell are YOU doing in here?" "I hear you turned your life around and that you were through with all this madness, is that true?" he asked. "What's up Lil Ray?" "I need to see you for a minute." I wasn't there to have casual conversation. I told him what I needed and fifteen minutes later, I had both—a nine and a thirty eight. I was ready. Like I said, it didn't take me long to resort back to my grimy days. I was in total hood mode at that point. "I'm gonna take care of this Brianna," I said. "I am not going to let him get away with this baby. I wasn't there to protect you, but I will get my own brand of justice for your death and our child's death. He will never rest comfortably again, that's a promise." It's like I could hear Brianna telling me not to do it. To let the police deal with it. She just didn't want to see me in any trouble.

Again I would have to disappoint her.

I picked up Darryl from work that evening and told him to drop me off at this Motel where I was going to stay for a few nights. I didn't want to stay with any family or friends, because I did not want to drag anyone else into what I was about to do. I checked into the motel under another name. It was a little hole in the wall, and they didn't care about seeing ID or anything. Basically, it was a spot where hookers took their dates. No one paid too much attention to it, so it was perfect.

Around ten o'clock I called a taxi to take me to 'Ordinary Places'. When we arrived, I asked the driver to wait a few minutes while I went to see if someone I was looking for was inside. When I walked in, there were naked women everywhere, and all I could focus on was this guy's face. I walked all around the entire club and didn't see anyone who even came close to looking like him. On my way out, I asked the bouncer at the door if he knew this guy (I began to describe him) "From your description you are looking for Reggie Swain. He's a regular, but he is not in tonight. If I see him is there something I should tell him?" he asked. I felt like shooting HIM right in his face for asking me that. "Yeah, if you see him, just tell him a friend dropped by." "What's your name?" he asked. I just walked out. Now it was off to 'The Chateau'.

The taxi driver was cool. He actually had me smiling telling me stories of people who has been in his cab and the crazy things he's been through. I was trying to be nice, but I just wanted to get to this club. Fifteen minutes later we pulled up. Again, I ask him to wait as I investigate who was in there. As I walked in, I noticed that this place had more class than the other joint I was just in. It was also easier to see everyone in there. As soon as I got searched by the bouncer, (yes, with both guns) and walked in, I spotted him! He was sitting at the bar and had a young lady sitting on his leg. I went back outside and paid the taxi driver and told him that he could leave. I went back inside and took a seat at a table near the rear of the club, but with a very good view of my target. I must have sat there for two hours, drinking cokes one after the other and being approached for 'private dances' by a few of the girls. The whole time my eyes were on him. He was not walking out of this club without me on his behind. I kept thinking as I watched him...trying to get the pictures out of my mind of him raping and beating Brianna the way she was beat, then choking her to death! The longer I sat looking at him, the more I wanted to just go over, but the barrel his temple and just pull the trigger, but I had to be smart. I did not want to go to jail, I just wanted revenge. He stole from me, and he has to pay.

The hours passed and it soon came closing time. Some of the girls that had come over to me throughout the night, were getting dressed in the back and coming out in their street clothes.

That's how I knew it was about to close. My target was sitting there in a grey business suit throwing around a whole lot of money, and the women were eating it up. He obviously was a big deal, to himself! Maybe that's the reason why he got so angry at Brianna. He wasn't a big deal to her I bet. She probably pissed him off because she wasn't for sale. He appeared to be the type of guy that was spoiled and if he didn't get his way, he would get angry. I picked all this up about him just by sitting there observing him for the past 3 hours. Where was I going to do this? I didn't want to do it in here, too many witnesses. Since everyone was leaving, I would wait for him outside. I walked outside and stood across the street from the club.

As I leaned beside a telephone pole, in front of a restaurant, I heard a voice. "Jay, why haven't you learned your lesson yet baby? You are about to do something that is going to have major consequences and it is not even worth it now baby. I'm gone! I'm not coming back! You killing him will remove you from this world just like he removed me!" Tears began to trickle down my face. "I hear you Brianna, but I can't let him get away with what he did to us. HE MUST PAY!" I stood outside for at least forty minutes. Most of the cars in the parking lot were gone. Only three remained. One I assume belonged to Reggie. The next thing you know, he came walking out with a very pretty black woman. They kissed in front of her car then he walked her around to the drivers side, took her key and opened the door for her. What a gentleman! He leaned in and kissed her again before she started up the car. As she backed up, he stood there waving. Just as she pulled out of the driveway, I walked across the street with both hands in my hoodie pockets in front of me. I had the hood on. "Excuse me sir, can I ask you a question?" "I don't talk to hoodlums," he said, drunk out of his mind. "Oh, you're gonna wanna talk to me." I pulled back the hoodie as I took the nine out of my right pocket and pointed it at him. "What the hell are you doing? Who the hell are you? Do you want my money…here, take it!" He looked young, but sounded groggy like an old eighty year old man. "I don't want your money partner! As a matter of fact, you took something from ME, and even though I can't get it back, you are about to know the pain you put her through in her last hours." "Did you know she was pregnant?" I asked. "I don't know what the hell you're talking about…who is she? Hey, don't I know your face from somewhere?" he had the nerve to ask. "Yeah partner, from the airport when you confronted my fiancée a few weeks before you raped and killed her the other night." "Oh, you mean the bitch!" he said. "So, you were the reason she just wouldn't give it to me huh? Because she was so in love with YOU? I didn't pay YOU that much attention in the airport because all I wanted was her. All she had to do was spend time with me, and it wouldn't have happened. That bitch deserved what she got. She thought she was too good for me. Can you imagine that? Too good for ME?" (Pop) went the first shot. I shot him in his leg and he hit the ground. "Now what, you want to kill me too?" he asked. "and spend the rest of your life in prison? All for a bitch! (pop) second shot "Aaaaaaaaaaa..wait a minute!" he pleaded. The second shot was right between his legs. If he does live, he'll never use that again! Now he was crawling on the ground. One hand on his leg and the other between his legs. Blood was everywhere. "So now you know what torture feels like huh big man? You don't look so big now. (pop) another shot. This time in his behind. "STOP, PLEASE STOP SHOOTING ME! I'LL CONFESS TO THE KILLING! PLEASE, DON'T KILL ME. I'M SORRY…. I JUST COULDN'T TAKE IT THE WAY SHE JUST KEPT TELLING ME NO. WOMEN DON'T TELL ME NO. THAT'S WHY I DID WHAT I DID TO HER…. TO TEACH HER A LESSON. I DIDN'T MEAN TO KILL HER! SHE PUNCHED ME IN MY FACE AND I JUST LOST CONTROL! PLEASE!" By this time, he was good and sober. I was standing over him with the gun pointed at his face. "I would tell you to tell my fiancée and my child that I said hello and that I got you for them, but you're going in the opposite direction." (pop) the final shot, right to his fore-

head. It was done. It was over. My life as I knew it was over. Hell, it was over when I found out about Brianna's murder, but now it was REALLY over, and I didn't feel a bit of remorse.

I tossed the gun in the bushes and ran…and just kept running. I threw the other gun in the sewer as I ran. I could hear police sirens in the distance.

I guess whomever was the last person to leave the bar, must've heard the gunshots and called the police.

I made my way back to the motel I was staying at, ripped off my bloody clothes, and took a shower. "Now you've done it!" I heard a voice say. "Why Jay, why did you have to go and do that?" "You have people in your life that need you! What can you do for ANYONE behind bars?" "I know you love me Jay, and I loved you too—more than you can ever, ever imagine." "I'm sorry Brianna," I said crying. "I'm sorry that I was not here for you baby!" "I'm sorry I let that animal hurt you and our child." The room got cold and I swear it was Brianna's spirit. I felt something touch me and I opened my eyes. It was the police. The parking lot where I just killed this man had cameras and the owner watched the whole thing on video tape. So did the police. They saw which way I ran and didn't take long after that to find me.

It was no sense on calling anyone. The Judge probably wouldn't even set bail for me. I went there with the intent to kill him. They could question the taxi driver, the bouncer from the first club, the bouncer for the second club who saw me when I came in. There were too many people who knew I was after him. I had to take what I had coming to me like a man.

I was allowed to go to the funeral. The first one I have ever been to, and I was in shackles. Although to me it was a disgrace to be at my fiancée's funeral in shackles, everyone there understood why I was and no one held it against me.

About seven months went by before my trial. My time in county jail was pretty easy being that I knew mostly everyone in there. It was sorta like being out on the streets, but with restrictions. My mom hired the best lawyers money can buy. I pleaded guilty to manslaughter and was sentenced to 15 years to life, but with good behavior I could be out in 6 years.

Every waking moment I thought about Brianna. Don't get me wrong, I thought about others too…my children, my mom, Mrs. Williams, the fellas, Zora, Mr. Levin, but mostly about Brianna and my unborn child. Who would have thought that only a year ago I was happily single with a great job, a loving mom, friends that I enjoyed being around and in total control of my heart. In no way do I regret meeting Brianna, but I wasn't expecting it. I wasn't expecting to fall head over heals in love. Not me! I wasn't gonna let that happen. The way I saw it, love was overrated. Why fall in love if you can have just about anything you want from a woman, any woman, many women, without all that's attached to love. Until I met Brianna Williams. She changed my life and I will always love her for that. She showed what a wonderful thing love can be. Loving Brianna took my heart places it had never been before, and I wasn't afraid.

Most importantly, I know I disappointed God. I had known better. I didn't have to do what I did. I knew enough and had enough evidence against this person that it would have only been a day or two before he would have been in police custody and soon after, justly convicted of one of the most horrible crimes imaginable…and I would still have my freedom, but I dealt with things the only way I was taught to deal with things. I didn't follow God, I followed self. It's a painful lesson, but so is love. In retrospect, I ask myself was a love that I had never known, had never opened myself up to, one that I finally allowed in, really worth it? Brianna was worth it! Every minute, every second!

All I can do now is write. I know its wild how things happened, how things turned out. I know you're probably sitting there saying I should have listened to Brianna when she was trying to explain to me. You probably wondered how I could not even want to take her calls, to just listen to her. Or maybe you're wondering why it took me so long to find out what she did for a living! I know we men are strange creatures (a woman once told me that) She said men were harder to figure out than Chinese arithmetic. Understanding a man is a mystery that will go down in history as 'unsolved'. Yeah, I would say that it's gonna take centuries to figure out what really goes on—"INSIDE"…the mind of a man!

Chapter 20

Jailhouse Poetry

As I glance through the tiny window that connects me to the outside world, people walking, cars passing, buses still polluting the air...but I'm in here. A desperate act triggered by revenge led me to my end. Now with a roomy—I got the state trying to sue me...prosecutors wanting death, wanting me to breathe my last breath—all because I lashed out. At a fool without conscience, blasted em in the face with the nine from my waist because he caused me pain that stuck like a knife, took my childs life—raped and murdered my wife...who's the victim here?

I beg for God to forgive my actions, please lord don't hold me accountable I was enraged in a pure fit of passion. All I could see was red...visions of bloodstains still in my head. Tears ran down my face as I put the hot pistol back in my waist...when is it gonna stop?

The voices that talk to me nightly, daily they greet me...I try to stop em' but they keep fighting me! Brianna in one ear, my unborn child in the other—then it's my children, my friends, Zora and my mother. Why try to tell me what kind of fool I am, what I lost what I had, why didn't I just think...why'd I have to be so mad? The actions of one can cause pain to many, but at that time, there were no thoughts of any...one but me and my gun and the reason I was there...to seek revenge for my baby. Both of em!

Now I sit with a plastic knife trying to cut through my bread the same way I cut through life, with no rhyme or no reason living like love had no meaning, hurting destroying all that was in my path, the self glorification sometimes kicked my ass. But I knew no better...I was raised like man still wearin' my childhood sweater. Masking all my feelings thoughts and emotions I couldn't let love get the best of me...Until Brianna.

Bri you came into my life like a thief in the night and took the very essence of my soul...like it belonged to you. Happy, successful but still missing a part going into my thirties like a Grinch I had no heart. But you came and you showed me that it was Ok, let go and allow God to carry me to a place where only few couples are blessed enough to go...yet I didn't know. Cause when it all came down to it, I spit on your feelings and shoved you aside like a broken down ride...and I fell short.

You called for me, you needed me your soul reached out to touch me and only came back empty. But I felt you Brianna. I knew every thought you had, I felt every breath you would breathe. Every time you reached out to touch me grasping at air...mad and upset because I wasn't there. Your last night on this earth, I tossed and turned like I was giving birth...the uneasy feeling that I had—though I couldn't image it being this bad.

I never got the chance to tell you that I'm sorry. I'm so, so sorry baby. As a man...your man, I failed you. But at the same time I want to thank you. Thank you for your love, the love that you shared with me so freely. God truly shined on me when he allowed you to enter my life. My ray of sunshine...you were everything to me Brianna, and if I could do it all over again, I would love you even more. You taught me not to run from love, but to stand and face the challenges of life, and even though you're no longer here...you'll always be my wife.

Mom forgive me for my selfish actions, it wasn't my plan to place your heart in traction. You were there for me in so many ways...so many days when I couldn't do it alone, you don't even know it but just picking up the phone was the remedy that cure all, you're my mom...be proud, stand tall. I'm still your son and my love for you still remains, forever untouched like the cross where Jesus was chained. Tell my family that I love them and that they are in my prayers...my brothers my sister and anyone else who cares.

My children—my love for you is the greatest thing I've ever felt...your dad is gonna be gone for a while, but I want you to know that my heart carries a smile, in such a short time that we've had each other, you two have taught me more about love than I could have ever learned from any woman.
I have an Agape love for you that will never be matched...it will never, ever be lessened, no matter how many years till I come back.

Look out for each other and Keep God in your lives, he will deliver you good families, a loving husband my daughter and for you my son, a loving wife. Your dad is not dead, I'm just locked away and I'll tell you this much cause it's true, killing a man is a sin against God but the real crime is that I wont be there for you.

I pray one day that I'm forgiven, please God show favor on my soul. I'm still your child father. I still need you. I'm sorry for disobeying what I know to be your commandments. I love you father...I love you for bringing Brianna into my life. For allowing me the chance to dance one last dance with love. To finally feel what is real inside...what you placed there 30 years ago, that I would never know...until now. True love...its such a beautiful thing, and only you can bring that feeling. I know now that one could never know that its impossible to show without knowing you...you are the captain of my ship and even though I failed, even though I slipped…you're still in command. Love me, protect me…until the day when you call me home, to meet Brianna and my child that I've never known.

You've blessed me in a way that most will never understand….
Now all I can do is keep writing…..about what's on the "INSIDE" of the mind of this man!!

About the Author

New to the writing scene, Stacey Green has goals to be next on the set of young, expressive African American writers to capture an audience with his bold and straightforward insight into the thinking of the average black man looking for love. Born and raised in Elizabeth, New Jersey now residing in Atlanta Georgia, Stacey was born the youngest by ten years of four children. He grew up making his own rules his own way which caused a lot of pain and misery. When it came to women, he could never understand women and they could never understand him. Writing has always been a way to express himself and writing this book has helped him a great deal mentally and emotionally. He is currently a counselor at a College in Atlanta and a member of New Mercies Christian Church in North Georgia

He is currently writing his second book titled: "Daddy Don't" which tackles a very sensitive subject in today's world, especially the African American community. Look for it's release in the fall of 2006.

Definitely look for more from him in the future.

978-0-595-39421-0
0-595-39421-3

Printed in the United States
60875LVS00004B/40